CAHOKIA TREMBLES

THOMAS SABEL

Cover designed and created by Elizabeth Kramer

Printed by CreateSpace

Available from Amazon.com and other retail outlets.

First printing, 2018.

"One of the greatest cities of the world, Cahokia was larger than London was in AD 1250."
Cahokia Mounds State Historical Site
(https://cahokiamounds.org/about/)

"Cahokia Mounds, some 13 km north-east of St Louis, Missouri, is the largest pre-Columbian settlement north of Mexico. It was occupied primarily during the Mississippian period (800–1400), when it covered nearly 1,600 ha and included some 120 mounds. It is a striking example of a complex chiefdom society, with many satellite mound centres and numerous outlying hamlets and villages. This agricultural society may have had a population of 10–20,000 at its peak between 1050 and 1150. Primary features at the site include Monks Mound, the largest prehistoric earthwork in the Americas, covering over 5 ha and standing 30 m high."
UNESCO World Heritage Site
(http://whc.unesco.org/en/list/198)

"There are historical accounts of major earthquakes in the New Madrid region during 1811–12. The geologic record of pre-1811 earthquakes also reveals that the New Madrid seismic zone has repeatedly produced sequences of major earthquakes, including several of magnitude 7 to 8, over the past 4,500 years. . . The preponderance of evidence leads us to conclude that earthquakes can be expected in the future as frequently and as severely as in the past 4,500 years." (USGS Fact Sheet *Earthquake Hazard in the New Madrid Seismic Zone Remains a Concern*)

Chapter 1

Something in the bearded young man's pronunciation of his single syllable last name—"Thrace"—caught Dr. Troy Broadspeare's ear when he first called the roll.

"Thrace? It's Thrace, isn't it?"

The student nodded.

"Would you be kind enough to let me hear you speak? You'll have to do it sometime this semester." A mild twittering rustled from the back rows. Broadspeare immediately regretted making a joke at the student's expense.

"What would you like me to say?"

"Anything you'd like. What's your major? Why you are here? Why you want to go to college? Maybe something about your family. It helps us to get to know one another." Broadspeare softened his voice to sound as conciliatory as possible. He moved to the front of the desk and sat on it, hoping this act of informality would put the young man ease. All the while, the student had been flipping through the syllabus as if looking for some secret panel tucked in among the assignments through which he might escape.

"Business major. And I'm taking this class because it meets on Tuesdays and Thursdays and fills in an elective requirement. That enough, Professor?"

"And you're from Oklahoma, but not originally. You were born in your mother's country—Slovenia, and spent your first two years there followed with three years in upper New York state living with your father's family on their dairy farm. You moved to Oklahoma where you attended a Lutheran grade school and then a public high school."

The student fell back in his seat, ignoring the syllabus that had dropped to the ground. The rest of the class leaned forward, watching the student's expression go from disinterest to rapt attention.

"How... how did you know about the dairy farm?" he stammered.

"That was an educated guess. Everything else came from you, from the traces of accents, the way you form the sounds with the shape of your mouth and placement of the tongue, from the breathing and rhythms of speech. The way we speak delivers our personal histories—where we lived, who we lived with, the schools that influenced us. It's all in our speech. And all we have to do is listen and pay attention. This is part of what our study of linguistics is about."

In the pause that followed, an energetic girl in the back row shot up her hand, waved it vigorously, and called out, "Professor Broadspeare! Me. Now me!"

He glanced at her and clipped off, "Louisiana, St. Leona Parish, public school, one summer vacation in the Provence of France."

She dropped her hand and blushed at her transparency.

As he walked across the campus, Broadspeare congratulated himself that he hadn't been caught up in the moment and spilled everything he had discovered about the student... What was his name? Fred, probably Anglicized from Fedya—Thrace. There was a touch of a federal penitentiary in there picked up from his father and blurting that out could have harmed the young man.

"Troy!"

He stopped and turned. Dr. Avon Greenefield, easily recognized with the gentle elegance of years that seemed to have passed her by, leaving little effect.

"Did you get your hair cut for the new semester?" he said. "Short hair looks good on you."

"There's no need to flatter an old married woman, Troy."

"I'm not, not really. Maybe a bit, after all, my review for tenure is coming up."

"And that's what I wanted to remind you of. I've sent another email. Be sure to read this one, will you? You must have skipped over my last one about the curriculum meeting. You were sorely missed."

"It must have gotten buried among all the others that flood in from every office on campus. Why does the administration have to tell me everything that goes on? It all comes across like academic spam."

"I won't disagree with you on that, but you need to be more mindful, Troy."

She stopped, and he followed her lead, and they both stood in the middle of the sun-drenched courtyard. "It's a beautiful day for the start of the semester. God has certainly blessed us with this one."

Troy didn't like it when she went pious on him. He knew she reserved her religious comments for intimate friends, and he was thankful for that, but not so thankful as to call upon the name of a god he didn't believe in. His grandmother had tried to stuff him with churches during the summers he stayed with her. Only the music made any sense to him. Give me something solid, like the rocks under our feet, he would have said to her if they were arguing religion. All he could reply to Greenefield was, "Yes, it is beautiful. But since we are in Kansas, it won't stay that way long."

"Then, Dr. Broadspeare," she announced, "enjoy it while you can. And don't forget to look for my email."

When they parted company, a cloud crossed in front of the sun, casting gloom over his path. He didn't want to go to his office, that tiny, windowless basement room of painted cinder block. It was an industrial sort of room, not at all like those of some of his previous professors and especially not like those at the University of Navarre. But then Kansas Eastern University is a far cry from the 500-year old university where he studied under Dr. Nashure Keene. Keene had opened his eyes, and especially his ears, to the wonders of litholingquistics, the study of the effect of plate tectonics and other subterranean rock movements on human speech.

"It's not the music of the spheres, it's the grumbling of the ground!" Keene would exclaim in the classroom. "All language is nothing more than vibrations, the pulsing waves of air that move from the speaker to the ears of the hearer. But where did this start? And what influences every language ever spoken or will be spoken? The movement, the vibrations of the stones beneath our feet. Listen to them, and you will hear all the languages ever spoken in that place. Why are there so many languages and dialects? Why do the Scots speak English one way, and the Americans of the Great Plains another? The subtle vibrations that rise up from the ground and command the throat to echo back the sound. Go to a place where the plates rub against each other and you will hear and recover the dead languages of mystery."

Broadspeare followed Keene through the hills of Tuscany, working with a device Keene called his litho-stereoscope. They examined the deepest crypts of ancient churches, trying to match the shifts of the stones with the rhythmic pulses of the church choirs singing above them. They listened to the walls of Etruscan tombs, listening and amplifying the slightest variations and applying that to the mysterious script the Etruscans left carved on the tomb walls. Keene was certain he was getting close to the solution when, one day, the walls of the tomb collapsed, killing him. Troy had told not to go into the tomb alone, but to wait until he had returned from his errand, but the old man left a note saying he couldn't wait, not after getting this close. The collapse also crushed the litho-stereoscope. While Troy had the original plans of the device, Keene had made so many adjustments and alterations that they were as good as useless. At the loss of his mentor—and the only one who truly understood his doctoral thesis—the university was hard-pressed to present him his doctorate, but finally did so more on the reputation of Keene than Broadspeare's scholarly work.

It was not as a litholinguist that Greenefield hired him, but as an English teacher with occasional classes in linguistics. What had put him over the top were his diplomas which boasted an Ivy League school—Rutgers, a British one—University of Leicester, and the European doctorate, all of which looked very good in the promotional literature. That he had a specialty in an obscure, if not specious, field of study, she conveniently buried. She had to come like this young man who quickly developed a positive rapport with his students. If only his journal articles were better.

One of these journal articles faced Troy when he entered his office. The bright glare of the fluorescent light off the white cinderblock walls hurt his eyes. Even bringing in his own office furniture—a mismatched collection of wooden pieces he had gathered catch-as-catch-can dulled the institutional feeling only a bit. He quickly turned on an incandescent lamp on the desk and turned off the overhead. He had ignored the email that prohibited the use of incandescent bulbs in the name of energy efficiency with the comment, "How can I be efficient under the glare of these interrogation lights?"

He sat down, turned on the computer, and pulled up the file on the article he had been researching for the past nine months. The work had been going nowhere. He had been studying the maps of recent earthquake activity in the eastern Mediterranean, laying over maps of dialects, and listening to hours of recordings: archived radio and television programs that he compared to current ones. He didn't hear much difference. Fortunately, many of these languages were ones he didn't know, so the meaning didn't distract him. All the while the nagging question persisted. What if Keene, whom he had admired and loved was full of . . . manure. (He couldn't bring himself to think the common term.) What if all this was nonsense? He put on the headphones and listened for ten more minutes.

He couldn't pay attention to anything he heard. It melted into gibberish and noise. *This has all been a damned waste of time, like the years chasing after that crackpot Keene and his cockamamie theories. And what the hell am I doing stuck in Kansas?* He stopped, tore the headphones from his head and threw them across the room, nearly taking the computer with it.

Email. He might as well check that. Avon's message should be there.

If the first one on the list could have been written in fire, it would have been. The sender used all the elements of urgency that could be conspired: red letters in all caps, redundant exclamation points, and flags. The letter came from the editor of the journal yet to be written article was for. The politeness of the greeting didn't match the subject line.

"My dear Dr. Broadspeare," it began. Troy read that they were holding up the press for him, reminding him for the fourth time that his deadline had passed, and that they had to have his article by the end of the week. An added postscript informed him that the journal was increasing its editorial fee and that the amount he needs to submit through PayPal, when he sends his article, should reflect this change. "Thank you very much, and we have appreciated working with you. Dr. Agnimukha Haidar Ravanna, Lahore, Pakistan."

Reading fee. Nothing more than a vanity press for scholars who need publication points. And that's what I've become. I'll give them what fits their bill and mine.

He went back to the file of the article. He had first gone at it filled with a firm belief in his theories, but his interest had faded months ago. Procrastination now pushed his back to the wall of desperation, opening the door to the brotherhood of those students he had failed in their desperate acts of shoddy scholarship. He pulled from beneath the stack of unread papers he had crammed into the bottom desk drawer his secret solution, a book his sister had given to him on the first anniversary of his divorce as a wry joke. It was called

"The Joy of Lex" and it contained a collection of games and puzzles about words and their meanings. His first intention was to put it on the Goodwill pile, like so many of his sister's off-color gifts, until he found the Gobbledygook Generator on page 178. This was a listing of words laid out in three columns that the pained writer could combine to create high sounding phrases of fluff. He had long been aware of its temptation, more as a joke, he had told himself, to put something over on his colleagues, but it had been a temptation never acted upon. The generator, like all temptations, worked its way into his soul and lingered there until now.

He opened it to page 178 and lay the open text next to the keyboard. The dull opening of the sentence "This paper is about…" was quickly transformed into a mind-numbing "This paper seeks the gradual conglomerative structure of the compatible polarity within the linguistic calculus bearing upon the elitist usurpative phase of the algorithmic simulacrium." Within an hour the seven required pages were completed, and he had no idea what he had written. But then, the chances of anyone reading it were next to nothing. He attached it to the email response to Ravanna, pulled up the PayPal account and all but drained it, depriving him of his secret stash built from the pitiful inheritance his mother had left him when she was killed in a freak accident while accompanying his father on an archeological dig in Syria. The inheritance came from an Accident Death policy banks give with the first $1,000 provided for. She had upped it to five thousand and had named him the beneficiary, much to everyone's surprise. Perhaps it had been a way of making up for the guilt of the motherhood she bore like a cross. This article's fee depleted his legacy.

With Ravanna's fire extinguished, he plowed through the rest of the emails, deleting them in mass while keeping an eye opened for Avon's. She hadn't sent it yet and the rest of the university news bored him more this semester than it did in the past. Particularly annoying were those from anxious students more concerned about their grades than if they might learn anything. At least Thrace had been refreshingly honest with him. He reminded the anxious students to read the syllabus again.

He had highlighted nearly an entire page of email and was about to hit DELETE when one from a different school caught his eye. He didn't recognize the sender or the URL. The subject line gave the title of his dissertation: Telluric Traces. He hadn't paid much attention to that in the past six years, and neither had anyone else. As far as he knew less than 20 copies had been distributed and those were in university libraries cheerfully gathering dust along with countless other dissertations.

Dear Dr. Broadspeare,

Before I introduce myself, let me thank you for the insightful and ground-breaking work you have done with Telluric Traces. (God, this is laying it on pretty thick. What in heaven's name do they want?) *I am a graduate student* (of course, who else would bother to read it.) *at Illinois University at East St. Louis majoring in English. Since I will be doing research into the field of litholinguistics, I am hoping that you would be available to answer a few questions should they arise while I pursue this fascinating and overlooked topic.* (Overlooked? How about despised and ridiculed.)

Sincerely,
Welsey Yergens.

Well, Welsey—what a name—what should I do? If I respond, how deeply would all this play out? It's not like I don't already have enough to do.

The phone in his pocket vibrated once, probably a text from Sarah. That's the last thing I need, another entanglement with a female grad student. "Sorry, Welsey," he said to the screen, "You'll have to stick to my journal articles if you want more answers." He pushed the key and Welsey disappeared. He pulled the phone from his pocket, noticing that he had to stand to tug it free. Time to lose weight. He stood by his desk and read the message. It began with the nickname she had placed on him, which wasn't a good sign. She was about to make demands on him and his time, some sort of errand or problem he had to come and solve. Before he continued reading the message, he looked at the photograph of them taken two years before when they celebrated their first anniversary of her moving into his house. He had placed the photo in frame that had been a wedding present from a distant friend and once held his wedding picture. He picked it up and tried to recall both the friend's name and what his wife had looked like.

The Sarah Mosier who looked out from the picture looked younger than her years, making him look older even though the difference in their ages wasn't as much as most might guess. Their relationship began when she was one of his graduate students. She was a returning adult student and, if it were not for his wife's recent abandonment of him for her native Indonesia, she might have caught his eye. As it was, he possessed no inclination towards any relationship. Nine months had to pass before he was able to look at a woman and the one he spied was Sarah, remembering her as a bright student with more maturity than most.

He turned the photograph to better catch the light from the desk lamp. A shadow fell across it, aging her to her current appearance. If the same photo were taken today, he would have looked younger. He set it down and returned to the text message. His insight into her pattern didn't fail him. It was a list of items to pick up on the way home, along with a reminder that the guest toilet was stopped up and he needed to do something about it. He replied with the letter K, resigned to his duties.

Broadspeare grabbed a few files along with some books, threw them into his shoulder bag, and headed out the building. He wasn't planning to do anything with them. They were an excuse to carry something and give the appearance that he was hard at work. The courtyard that he and Avon had crossed that morning was filled with students enjoying the weather. He paid special attention to the young women in their short-shorts and U-neck tank tops. He stopped staring when he realized that it was biologically possible that some of these could have been his daughter. The thought made him feel old.

His late model car reinforced that feeling. He had bought the Taurus wagon when he and his wife moved to Kansas, needing the space to carry their worldly belongings, the kind of car designed with a family in mind and cushy enough for grandparents. He no longer took pride in the fact that it had more than 100,000 miles, but despite the rust, it continued to serve and provided transportation in a city lacking public transportation.

The hardware store took him three miles out of his way. Broadspeare had forgotten about the traffic and the side trip added thirty minutes. This time, he bought the most expensive plunger they stocked since the others had proven less than efficient for the stubborn plumbing. When he pulled into the driveway the height of the grass reminded him of the mowing he had put off.

This modest, two-story house in an older and settled neighborhood had been the undoing of his marriage. His wife's anger exploded when she discovered that they were not renting the house, but had bought it, and in thirty years it would be theirs forever. She had never liked Kansas and had accompanied Troy with the idea that the time in Kansas Eastern would be temporary until a better, more prestigious position was offered, like that of an Ivy League school, or better still, a European one. She never fit in, and outside of some freelance translation work, never found a job. The purchase of the house was the last straw. On the day Troy signed the mortgage papers, she left him, only to discover that she was pregnant. By the time their daughter was born, she was back with her parents in Jakarta, living off the family wealth. Only by happenstance did he discover he was a father, and while he tried to contact his wife, he never received a reply other than one from a lawyer informing him that on the account of his abuse and neglectful nature, no contact was permitted.

He should have sold the house, but the collapse of the housing market made that impossible. When Sarah moved in, it had become the nest of an educated bachelor. If a house could have been covered with tweed instead of ivy, it would have been this one. Books and papers stacked filled the corners. Dust covered the unused furniture and the walls bore the plain white of solitude. What Sarah had lacked in her earlier life, she tried to fill by bringing his home to a level of domesticity famous among homes on the Great Plains. For Troy, the novelty wore off in the first two years and now, the burden of tranquility calling for the need of repairs and lawn care clung like a toxic trumpet vine.

With shoulder bag in one hand and the clutch of plastic grocery bags in the other, he approached the door wondering which he would have to put down to get at his keys to open the door. He had slipped the keys into the left-hand pocket of his jacket, and he was right handed. Emptying both hands would solve the problem, but then he would have to pick up all the bags again, enter the house, set them down, close the door, and this whole process quickly grew into ODTAA— One Damned Thing After Another. The door opened before he could act.

Sarah opened the door and reached for the groceries. "Did you forget anything this time?"

"I hope not. I followed your text, at least as much as I could follow. Some of the abbreviations threw me."

She looked in the first bag and then the second. "What's this?" She pulled out a bottle of Lysol. "Why did you get this? You were supposed to get lettuce for the salad."

"I could run back to the store if I had to."

"Don't bother. You must be tired from the first day. Did it go all right?"

"I'm not tired. The first day is pretty much the same every semester—get the syllabus in their little hands and make sure everyone is in the right class. Is it me, or are the students getting younger?"

"It can't be you. They must be getting younger. You didn't pull your usual magic trick, did you?"

He noticed a touch of disdain in the way she said, "magic."

"If you mean, did I demonstrate the importance of careful listening as crucial for the science of linguistics because traces of our lives continue to be with us, then yes, I did."

"Like I said, a magic trick. You won't pull that on our guests, will you? Some people like to have their lives hidden from public exposure. And you come across like a pompous professor when you it."

"Guests?"

"For tomorrow's dinner. The library hired a new clerk and since I'll be working with her, I thought I should get to know her and her husband."

"Why? We've never done anything like this before."

"Honey…" The muscles on his neck clenched. He got ready for what was coming next.

"Honey, we've talking about this before—how we've become so closed up here. We don't go out anymore and it's only the two of us. Why not have friends?"

"Do you remember the last time we tried to make friends with the neighbors?"

"It wasn't my fault that you had to pull your magic trick on them?

"How was I to know that he never told her he was an illegal alien?"

"Try to be nice tomorrow, all right?"

He muttered a promise about being nice, shifted past her and carried his briefcase into the study. While his office on campus held to order and tidiness, his study gave way to chaos. Stacks of folders leaned against each other as they rose from the floor. Layers of papers covered the desk. The books on the shelves were stacked rather than lined up on their spines, with half of them facing the back of the bookcase leaving their contents a mystery. When Sarah first moved in, she offered to clean and organize the room. No, Troy protested. He told her he liked it this way. He had lied. The study had become a repository of unwanted mailings, papers students had written years before, and books that had been given to him—ones he promised to read but never did, along with copies of scholarly and professional journals he had long given up on, including those that had published his articles and provided him with complimentary copies plus subscriptions that kept arriving long past their renewal dates. It was a room to escape into with the excuse of work to do which also provided a window to stare out of, past the clutter and up into the treetops.

He plopped the briefcase on top of the pile of papers setting on the desk. There it would remain, untouched, until he picked it up the next day and headed back to campus. He sat in the desk chair, pulled open the oversized file drawer, and pulled out an Indian pale ale. He opened it and drank. On his last birthday Sarah had surprised him with a tiny refrigerator, but it sat, still in the box, under a pile of journals and papers.

Ever since his studies in England, he took his beer warm, and the ale's case fit neatly into the otherwise empty drawer.

The evening with their guests was a disaster. If Troy had been able to mingle with the clerk it wouldn't have been so bad. She was at that attractive age between Sarah and his students. All too quickly the evening fell into gender bound segregation that chained him to her husband. Troy knew the evening was going to been awkward one the moment the husband introduced himself as the new youth pastor at one of the megachurches that lay past the interstate. Throughout the evening Troy vacillated between cringing at the man's pseudo-Southern Baptist drawl and wondering if this was part of Sarah's journey to respectability. When he and Sarah went to bed that night, she clung to her edge of the bed with her back planted firmly against him.

By the first killing frost, Sarah had moved into the guest room and kept urging Troy to attend church with her. He went a few times but then made excuses about the semester having a heavier course load and extra committee work, so he would have to be on campus Sunday mornings because it was quiet and he could get more work done. This was one of the few times the basement office was actually inviting.

The quiet Sunday mornings gave him the opportunity to clear his email. The university's spam filter let in more and more, despite complaints from him, his department, and everyone else. During one of those cleaning binges the title of his dissertation appeared again, this time with the word "help" applied.

Dear Dr. Broadspeare,

I am not sure if you received my earlier email sent eight weeks ago, so I am sending this in the hopes you will receive it. As I mentioned before, I have been working with your dissertation to guide me through my own area of research that centers around the Cahokia, Illinois, area, with particular attention paid to the ancient mound city. Fortunately, by consulting many of your later journal articles (although I found the last one more confusing than others), I answered my previous questions. However, and this why I am writing you a second time, a phenomenon is occurring here which, according to your theory, should not be taking place. A very rapid linguistic change is taking place, much faster than a generational shift. Not only is this shift evidenced in the youngest population—as expected—but also in the eldest. Please, Dr. Broadspeare, could you help me develop a solution to the problem? For your study, I am including three MP3 files, one taken from the radio archives of 1962, one dating from 1996, and the third made last week. I anxiously wait for your response.
Sincerely,
Welsey Yergens

What kind of a name is Welsey, male or female? Over the past few years, Troy had noticed a gender conflation in the names of his students, and the name Welsey confused him more. He wished he hadn't deleted the earlier email because it might have given him more information. Since Sarah would be spending most of the day with her newly found church friends, he decided to listen to the files, after all, this Welsey had gone to all the trouble of sending them.

He expected the '62 radio broadcast to be the typically flat, unaccented Midwestern dialect taught by many of the broadcasting schools of the time. When he heard the nasal twang coming through his Koss headphones, he smiled. This Welsey knows what he or she was doing by finding an authentically local broadcaster. When he played the second, the smile broadened to a grin. He heard the same voice, making the comparison all that much easier. Welsey has read my articles after all. And the difference came through clearly even in the same word used in similar context. He sensed a change but couldn't be sure in which direction it was going, whether it was following the trends of the future or echoing the past. He fast-forwarded through it and played the third. His excitement broke at the sound of a completely different voice. The original announcer had probably died by now and the voice in the headphones belonged to a much younger person. He listened through it and then hit play again.

This time he closed his eyes, leaned back in his chair and focused on the sound, filtering out the meanings of the words. For a minute he thought he heard something, or was it that he wanted to hear something and had put it there?

He copied the file into his modified PAATS linguistic program that could more easily control the speed and adjust for tones and rhythm. He slowed the speed by twenty-five percent and played it. Nothing. Then by half. Maybe. Then down to a one-eighth of its original speed. He leaned into the sound, bringing his complete focus to the sound. There it was—a sound like a thrumming, or a rhythm, or a voice out of its time, an ancient sound. What had this Welsey latched onto? He played it again, but this time it was gone, whatever had been there. Snatching the headphones off his head, he jerked the plug from the computer and slammed them back into the drawer.

Well, Welsey, you had me going for a while. With that sort of name, he wondered who might be behind this for it smelled of an elaborate joke. Who wanted to make him look like a fool in front of the academic community? If it's too good to be true… But how did this come out of nowhere? It's all too perfect. And what about this Cahokia?

Googling "Cahokia" brought up the description of a town in Illinois, on the other side of the Mississippi from St. Louis. The town had been named was named for the Cahokia tribe of Indians who had been driven off to make room for white settlers. What he read cemented the idea that this Welsey was the creation of someone's imagination. He was about to exit the site when he spied the link to Cahokia Mounds State Park. He opened the link and walked in.

The map of an ancient city filled the screen. The city's monuments were built from enormous piles of earth with the largest, according to the map's legend, still existing. Surrounding the ancient city had been a wooden palisade, and beyond the city walls, the builders had created a ritual center the site called "Woodhenge" because a circle of pillars made from the trunks of enormous cedar trees created a map that marked the equinoxes as well as the longest and shortest days of the year. In its prime, the city was larger than London at that time.

So there is a Cahokia City. His doubts remained. This Welsey has done his or her research to create the joke. He searched his mind for who might want to send him off on this wild goose chase. He couldn't think of anyone in the English department. The tenured faculty had written him off as a crackpot who was a decent teacher and regular committee member when he wasn't harping on about litholinguistics. The only thing that sullied his reputation was taking up with Sarah after having been her instructor, not that anyone could blame him after his wife abandoned him when she rejected the community.

The essays he had to grade had not yet been touched other than being shuffled and set into stacks of five. The entire collection from three classes turned in simultaneously was overwhelming. Small bits of five was manageable. When he looked at the name on the first paper he groaned loud enough to be heard in the hallway, had anyone been there. As he read he cursed the open enrollment policy of the school. By the end of the first page only three lines lacked red inked corrections. If the rest were like this, he knew he was in for a long slog, like dragging a sledge through mud.

He forced himself to grade the other four in the stack before he rewarded himself with a breather. He put down his special grading pen, a large barreled fountain pen that had become a personal talisman, and massaged his right hand with his left, leaned back and his eyes wandered the bookshelf. There was his life, not only his dissertation but also the accumulation of articles. The dates on the journal's spines revealed a flurry of productivity in the years immediately after receiving his doctorate before the distance between the dates lengthened and the quality of the journals declined.

He grabbed the second stack of five and attacked with his pen. Once, he had leaned towards leniency, but now he verged on viciousness. Every flaw glared at him—every grammar error, every misplaced comma, every trailing of faulty logic and lack of organization—all fell under the blood colored ink. The anger he felt towards that jokester Welsey fell upon the innocence of the students. His anger fired such energy that he finished the grading in half the time normally taken. No one in his classes received an A.

Grading done, he turned the computer back on and pulled up the email. Welsey Yergen's letter hadn't vanished. He passed on the temptation to delete it and then empty the deletion file. *What does this jokester want from me? If I delete it, I'll probably get another one.* He could think of no reason why he shouldn't reply, why he shouldn't play along.

Dear Welsey Yergens:

Please accept my apologies for not responding to your first inquiry, but my current research, and with the demands of faculty duties, have held my attention to the point that all else had to be excluded. I appreciate your having read my dissertation and subsequent articles. In regards to your request, I sadly must tell you that I need to say no at this time. I wish you great success as you apply my techniques in litholinguistics to the situation in Cahokia.
Sincerely,
Troy Broadspeare, PhD

He hit send, believing this would be the end of the matter. *The jokester has been put to bed and the joke done.*

The air had turned cold and the gray skies carried warnings of the first snow. Soon he would have to haul out his boots and the rest of the paraphernalia that accompanied winter in the Great Plains. He turned the car's heater on high and drove home, hoping the house would be empty.

It wasn't. Not only was Sarah's car there, so were two others, blocking the driveway. He parked on the street, got out, and slammed the door so hard the noise echoed off the front of the house. The front door flew open and Sarah, along with the youth minister, his wife, and another couple he had never met rushed out looking up and down the street.

Sarah looked at Troy and said, "We heard a bang and thought someone must have had an accident."

"No accident, just me wondering who was blocking the driveway."

The youth minister walked towards Troy, arms open as if to show he was unarmed. "I'm sorry, Troy. Sarah said you wouldn't be back until later. We weren't planning to stay as long as we did."

The other man approached with his hand extended. "You must be Troy. I'm James Shaeffer, pastor of the church, but you can call me Pastor Jim." He continued to walk towards Troy keeping his arm extended. Troy locked his hands behind his back and rose up down on the balls of his feet. Pastor Jim stepped back and stood shoulder to shoulder with the youth minister, forming a phalanx of two men set to protect the three women who remained clustered near the front door.

"Sarah was telling me about the work you've done with ancient languages," said Pastor Jim. "Especially in trying to crack the mysteries of the Etruscans." He broke ranks with the youth minister and took a tentative step forward. Troy didn't move. "I've had some training in ancient languages too," Pastor Jim continued, "Greek and Hebrew."

"That's when I was too young to know better," Troy said. "Could you move your cars so I can park in my driveway and off the street?"

"We were just getting ready to go," said the youth minister, beckoning his wife with a tilt of his head. She and the other woman joined their husbands, got in their cars, and drove off in opposite directions.

"Why did you have to be so rude to them?" Sarah said. Troy ignored her as he parked his car in the driveway. After he got out, he examined the driver's side for any damage he might have caused by slamming it. Seeing none, he picked up his briefcase and walked past her into the house, expecting her to follow.

"Troy, I asked you a question. Why did you have to be so rude to them?"

"Come inside, the neighbors don't need to be part of this."

She followed him into the house and then the living room. On the coffee table lay pieces of Etruscan art he had saved from his days with Dr. Keene, along with a copy of his dissertation. He picked the book up and said to the cover, "You seem to be following me everywhere lately. You need to go back on the shelf where you belong." He slipped it into the empty slot on the bookcase and without turning away said loudly, "I'd appreciate it if you'd leave that on the shelf where it belongs, closed and gathering dust. There's especially no need to drag it out and parade it in front of guests."

"But, Honey…"

His neck muscles balled into their fist.

"Honey, I'm proud of you, don't you know that?" She went to his side and stroked his arm. "You know I love you and want only what is best for you."

He put his arm around her waist and drew her closer. She slipped in between him and the bookcase and wrapped her arms around his neck.

"I've been thinking," she said as she kissed his neck.

"About what?" he said, nibbling her earlobe.

"Don't do that," she said, pulling away.

He stopped nibbling but didn't let go of her.

"I've been thinking about us. We've been together for three years now, haven't we?"

"No, we've known each other for longer than that, even if you don't count the time when you were my student.

"That's not what I mean. It's been three years since…" She pulled away from him, took him by the hand and drew him to the couch, sat down, and patted the place beside her. "… since we started living together."

He sat down. She picked up his hand and placed it on her lap, slowly rubbing the back of it in the rhythm of her words. "Three years… Did you ever, Troy, in all that time think that maybe it wasn't right?"

He jerked his hand away. "This is coming from them, isn't it? They put this idea into your head, didn't they?"

"No, Troy. You're wrong. They never said anything about our living arrangement."

"It's an arrangement now, is it?" He jumped to his feet and stood over her. "Arrangement? Why don't you come right out with it. Say it!" He pulled her from the couch, grabbed her shoulders and shook her. "Say it, say it out loud."

"Troy, don't. Troy, what's wrong? I've never seen you this way."

He ignored her and kept shaking her. "Say it, Sarah, say that we're living in sin. That's the word you're afraid of, isn't it? You're afraid to say 'sin'. Well, I'm not. We're living in sin and we're a pair of God-damned sinners."

"Let go of me." She pulled away from him, slapping his hands off.

He pulled them back and looked at his hands. "That hurts. See." He showed her the blood coming from a gouge on the back of his hand. "Why did you have to go and cut me for?"

"I didn't mean to. My ring must have done it. I'm sorry."

He sucked the blood from his wound. "I'm sorry, too. I overreacted. Come here." He opened his arms and she accepted the invitation. She leaned her head back, baring her neck to the path he was making from her ear down her neck.

"Oh, Troy," she moaned as he eased her onto the couch.

Suddenly the house vibrated. He looked up to see a vase totter off the shelf and fall, breaking into shatters. Then it was over. They sat up and she asked, "What was that?"

"It felt like an earthquake."

"Who ever heard of earthquakes in Kansas? Tornadoes, yes, but not earthquakes."

"They're rare, but they happen. All sorts of fault lines run like spider webs through the rock foundations. This is the second one this month."

"I didn't feel it, not like this one."

"You wouldn't have. One of the guys in the Geology Department told me about it. He told me that there seems to be more seismic action than usual.

Nothing to worry about, though. Now, where were we?" He put his arms around her and returned his attention to her earlobe. She pulled away and stood up.

"Not now, Troy."

"When then? Tonight?"

"I don't know. All this has left me exhausted. I'm going to take a nap." He watched her go up the stairs and heard the floor creak beneath her feet as she entered the guest room she had taken over. Then came the unmistakable click of the door being locked.

The broken vase remained on the floor. At least it was nothing precious, not like a family heirloom, he thought while carefully picking up the shards.

Chapter 2

"Fault lines are the vocal cords of the earth and earthquakes are their speaking." This had been the title of the first major paper Broadspeare had delivered after receiving his doctorate. He spoke the title aloud whole cleaning up the mess of the broken vase. "I wonder what the ground might be telling us right now," he continued. He put the shards into a cereal bowl and carried them into his study. He set the bowl onto a stack of papers and hoped the stack wouldn't topple. He rummaged through the cabinet and pulled out a walnut case, scarred and needing polish, the brass corners dull with tarnish. The nameplate on the bore a name: N. Keene. He opened it to the collection of specially crafted tuning forks his old professor had left him after he died. They weren't tuned to the normal musical tones, but according to the wavelengths that Keene had devised to be the range of primitive speech, the tones closest to the tones of the lithosphere. Broadspeare lifted out the velvet case of forks and unrolled it on the desk, then he pulled out the carefully folded map that lay beneath the tray. Being careful not to tear it, he unfolded it. This had been Keene's ongoing project of mapping the entire earth, matching tectonic plates and sub-plates to their proper tones. Unfortunately for Broadspeare's sake, Keene's focus had been on Europe and the Middle East. Only in his last years, the years before his untimely death, did he turn his attention to North America, getting only as far as the Appalachian Mountains. Kansas remained an unknown.

Wondering if the memory of the harmonic vibrations remained in the shards, Broadspeare selected out the largest one, closed the case, and set the shard in the exact center of the case's cover. He picked up the most likely fork, struck it against the palm of his hand, and held the base to the edge of the case as Keene had taught him. The shard tingled for a moment and stopped. He put the fork back in the velvet case, studied the map, and selected the one for the Algonquin language group, and repeated the procedure. This time, his highly trained ear picked up the subtle response—sort of a sigh—that rose from the shard before it shattered.

Probably wasn't anything there. He dumped the shards into the wastebasket and followed them with the rest of the broken vase. "Well, Nashure, maybe you were just an old fraud who got caught up in your own nonsense like I did," he said while carefully refolding the placing it and the forks back into the case. "You had me going for a minute, you and that Welsey Yergens person."

He opened the drawer for a much needed Pale Ale and found the drawer empty, calling for a trip to the grocery. While at the grocery, he thought about Sarah and their relationship. Along with the ale, he picked up a bottle of wine she liked, a bouquet of flowers, and ingredients for her favorite meal. She was still sleeping, presumably, when she got home. He focused on the cooking and didn't hear her enter the kitchen.

"Who are the wine and flowers for?" she asked.

"You, who else could they be for?"

She sniffed the flowers and read the wine label, then she smiled. As she inhaled, her nose twitched. "What's that I smell?"

"Your favorite, liver and onions."

"You're doing all this for me, after what happened this afternoon?"

"A lot of mistakes were made this afternoon. I know this sounds like an empty excuse, but I've been under a lot of stress this semester. And I received the strangest email you could imagine."

"I'd like to hear about it. You can tell me over dinner."

With the flowers, the wine, and the dinner, it felt like old times. He relaxed, leaned back in his chair, and related everything Welsey had written.

"You're not going to go there, like he…"

"… or she…"

"… or she asks, are you?"

"It's probably a joke, some warped joke that someone is playing on me."

"Why would anyone want to play a sick joke like that? To get you chasing over to Illinois to find a lost city?"

"The city's real. And the world of academics can be vicious. Maybe somebody wants my job and this would be great way to get me out of the way. A lot of hungry PhDs are out there."

That night they washed dishes together, laughing away the day. When it came time for bed, he took her by the hand up the stairs. She turned to go into the guest room, but he pulled her back and together they went into the bedroom they had once shared. Between kisses, he noticed that she kept looking through the open door, across the hall, and into the guest room. When they made love, he felt that she was in that other room instead of being with him, and before he fell asleep, he saw her slip across the hallway into the guestroom and close the door.

In the classroom the next morning, he handed back the papers dripping with red ink. Shock and despair flowed through the room, increasing with each paper handed back while anger, grief, and frustration passed over the students' faces as they skimmed the notes Broadspeare had made.

"I'm rather disappointed with this assignment," he said. "But it isn't the end of the world. You have two remaining assignments along with your major exam." He took his place behind the podium and Thrace shot up his hand. "Yes, Thrace?"

"Dr. Broadspeare…"

Broadspeare picked up on the twinge of prison creeping in around the edges of the pronunciation of his name, a sign of desperation. Thrace cleared his throat of its prison's twinge and said, "Dr. Broadspeare, are you going to be holding your regular office hours today?"

"Yes, why?"

"If you don't mind, I'd like to meet with you."

Damn. That was the last thing Broadspeare wanted. He counted his office hours as uninterrupted time to read the news on the internet, to be alone. He picked up on the murmuring from the back of the room as students verified with each other their professor's office hours. Broadspeare looked over the class and realized he would be meeting with a crowd of them that afternoon.

"I'm not being mean. I'm being honest." This sentence, and variations of it, Broadspeare repeated to the covey of students who clustered around his office door after he had pulled them in, one by one. Maybe he was being mean as he turned a deaf ear to their pleas for mercy, their excuses, and in the case of one young woman with too much mascara, a flood of tears that drew black lines down her face. Pleadings for extra credit were met with the blandishment to raise the quality of their work for the next assignment. Between students he could hear their comments in the hallway, comments that he wasn't the professor they had started the semester with, or, from one male student, the rude comment that he probably wasn't "gettin' enough."

By the time the last student had gone, Broadspeare had convinced himself that he wasn't being mean; instead, he had been too lenient over the past three years and that he had built the reputation around campus as being an easy A and a pushover for a sad excuse. No more. He would be the rigorous instructor who dutifully stays on the job and raises the standards for the students. When he left for the day, his heart was set and nothing could budge him. Tenure was in sight and that would be that, and whoever was behind Welsey would have to go elsewhere to find a job. He had his and wasn't giving it up.

When he arrived home, Sarah was preparing his favorite meal. An unopened pale ale sat next to a glass on the table. Before he could put his briefcase in the study, she kissed him on the cheek, cementing the picture of domesticity with the living room cleaned and dusted with a new vase replacing the one broken by the earthquake.

"Do you want your beer in there or in here?" She stood in the doorway, now holding the open ale in one hand and the glass in the other. This question had never been asked before in that house. Broadspeare habitually drank his ale alone, in the study, and he wondered if she had plowed through his desk to find the brand.

"I've seen the empties in the recycling, so I picked some up for you on the way home," she said before he could ask.

"I guess I'll take it in here." He sat on the edge of the couch while she stood by his side and filled the glass. She handed it to him and set the bottle on a coaster on the table.

"Uh, thank you, I guess."

"You shouldn't be so shocked, Honey." His neck clenched in anticipation of the next sentence. "I'm just trying to take care of you, that's all. And I've been thinking about us."

"What do you mean 'us'?"

"As a couple, about our relationship."

Broadspeare had an idea where this was heading, and he wasn't sure if he wanted to go there.

"I remember what you said about your wife."

"Ex-wife."

"Yes, your ex-wife. How she ran off and didn't bother to tell you she was carrying your child."

"She couldn't stand Kansas."

"I'm not like that. This is my home. I'm a Kansas girl."

"Sarah, exactly what are you getting at?" He almost used the word "proposing" but stopped out of fear of that word.

"I was talking with Patty this morning."

He held up his hand and asked, "Patty?"

"Patty, you've met her, she's Bill's wife."

Confusion over the flurry of names hurled at him set his head spinning. Names were never his strong suite. It took him half the semester to learn his students' names which were forgotten within ten minutes of posting their final grades.

"Bill, the youth minister," she explained.

"That Bill and Patty. And what did she have to say?"

"She's concerned about us."

"How could that be, she barely knows us," he said, emphasizing "us."

"She knows me, and she's concerned about me, then. And our situation."

He felt it coming and didn't know if he wanted to stay in the comfort of the ale she had poured and the rest of the newly found domestic bliss Sarah attempted to create.

"Patty says that the Bible instructs women to take care of their men, and that if I would take on an attitude like that, our lives would be better. Not only better but blessed. That was the word she said, 'blessed'."

Blessed. That's not a word he'd heard often, at least not when he was involved in the discussion.

She sat down, snuggled up to him, and put her hand on his knee. "We could have a good life together, Troy."

"I may have to go."

She pulled away, "What do you mean, 'Go'?"

"Field work. Research in Illinois near St. Louis. I know what I said before about it being a joke, but I was wrong about Welsey, completely wrong." He told her about the new emails he had received, how Welsey had been active in the field research, had read all of his articles, and had sent the sort of recording he would have made on the site. As he spoke, his excitement grew. He jumped from the couch and prowled the room. He flushed with the possibility while his temples pounded. His nostrils flared as he breathed faster and faster. "Yes, this Welsey, whoever she or he is, may be onto something." He spoke not to Sarah, but to himself, loudly and convincingly.

"Honey." The word come out like the whine of a loose fan belt and stopped him in midstride. "Are you sure this is for real? What do you know about this person, if it is a person. Anybody can send anything over the internet. You don't know if it's true or not. They haven't asked for your bank information, have they?"

"No, and it didn't come from Nigeria, either."

"Please, sit down, and let's talk about this." She picked up the half-finished glass of ale and offered it to him. He took it and sat down. "Think of the life we could have together," she said before she kissed him. He kissed her back and the excitement raised by Welsey's emails twisted around the excitement over Sarah.

That Sunday, instead of hiding out in his campus office, he accompanied her to church. He offered apologies to Pastor Jim when he shook his hand after the service.

Monday's email inbox contained more than usual because he hadn't looked at it since the previous Friday morning. Three were more important than the rest— one from Dr. Greenefield, one from an editor of a bona fide journal, and the third from Welsey.

The editor's was a reply to a proposal for an article. Troy forced himself to read past the first words, "We regret to inform you ..." Not only did was his article rejected, he was informed that any other proposals would also be rejected. Too many questions, it seems, had been raised about Broadspeare's professionalism and scholarly rigor. The editors, peers in his field of linguistics, further rejected the validity of the entire field of litholinguistics, especially when they discovered that Nashure Keene's experiments couldn't be replicated leading some to reject litholinguistics as an area of study lacking academic rigor.

Greenefield's email was short and to the point, as hers usually were. She requested a private meeting in her office as quickly as their schedules allowed and that he needed to reply before the close of business that Monday.

Welsey's began with a plea for a reply, wondering whether or not he believed she was serious, especially considering the attitudes that had been developed against litholinguistics. She further explained she believed research into the events taking place in Cahokia, especially when backed up with Dr. Broadspeare's expertise would boost credibility in the linguistic community. And, she continued, the bout of earthquakes taking place along the New Madrid Fault may well be connected to what was going on. "In case you doubt me, check out my Facebook page," she added as a postscript. Troy noticed Greenefields' address copied in the heading. Welsey's email had been sent on Friday and he wondered if Greenefield's urgency had anything to do with this.

When Troy walked into Greenefield's office the following Wednesday, he had armed himself with all the information he could find on Welsey Yergents. Wesley was a woman, a young and attractive woman—at least I can finally use a pronoun. And with some African heritage, probably slave ancestry considering the part of the country she lived in. Graduated cum laude from Illinois University, double major in Native American Studies and English, and was currently a graduate student at Southern Illinois University. Further research revealed that she had been listed a either an author or contributor to four articles found in reputable journals.

"The door's open, Troy. Come in and have a seat." Troy stepped into an office that was as hospitable and attractive in an old-fashioned way that echoed its occupant, down to the bowl of mints sitting on the visitor's side of the desk. "Just set those files on the floor, if you don't mind." He carefully lifted them from the leather chair. "You don't have to be so careful with them. I only set them there to keep someone from dropping in and staying too long when I've got work to do. It's more polite than telling them to get out of the office. Would you like anything? Tea or coffee?"

He declined and instead helped himself to one of the mints.

"Then if you don't mind, I'm going to see if any coffee is left." She stepped out and when she returned, she closed the door behind her. "Coffee's all gone, more's the pity." She picked up a stack of folders from the chair opposite Troy, set them on the desk and sat down. With her hand resting on the folders she said, "These, however, are important, especially for you, Troy."

His mind raced over what their contents could possibly be. It certainly couldn't be about that business with the students the other day. The wheels of academia don't move that quickly.

"You know you should be coming up for tenure fairly soon, don't you?"

He nodded.

"When I hired you, Troy, I have to tell you, I went out on a limb for you. I knew nothing about your field of litholinguistics and nor did any of my colleagues. However, your credentials were solid and, at that moment, added a bit of prestige to the department, considering that the majority of my faculty attended state schools—good schools, mind you—but not with the prestige of yours. You were one of my bragging points, if you have to know."

"You just said that I *was* one of your bragging points, not that I *am*."

"You heard me correctly, as I knew you would. Troy, what has been happening lately? When you first arrived here, your work was phenomenal. The students gave you positive recommendations and your research was first class. I know you went though some difficult times when your wife left you. Then there was that bit with taking up with a student."

"She was a former student by two semesters."

"Former student. But still, taking up with her raised several eyebrows. Need I remind you that this is a rather conservative part of the country?"

The mint developed the sour taste of bile. He swallowed it, embarrassed at the loudness of his gulping. He felt like saying "No, Ma'am," and hanging his head. Instead, he reached for a second mint and fiddled with it, holding it between the fingers of one hand and pulling on the wrapper with the other, twisting it without unwrapping it.

"I tried to read the last article you published with that open source journal from Pakistan. What a work of padding and weak research. How they can call themselves peer reviewed is beyond me. I looked like an act of desperation on your part."

"Did you say there wasn't any more coffee?"

"Yes, it's gone. Do you need something?"

What he needed was a strong drink, but he knew better than ask for it. He told her he needed a drink of water and asked to be excused for a moment.

His feet felt dead, numb while he walked the hall to the drinking fountain, thankful that the classes were in session and the hallway empty. He took several gulps, squared his shoulders, and went back to Greenefield's office, making sure to close the door behind him.

"And then there's this." Greenefield took the top folder from the stack that she had moved to the desk. She opened it and turned it so he could see the copy of the email that Welsey had sent on Friday. From the thickness of the paper within the folder, he knew she also had copies of the other emails.

"Yes, there's that," he said. "At first I thought it was some kind of a joke. I know that litholinguistics is held in low esteem by most, and I thought that this was some attempt to get me going. I didn't bother to answer the first one. If it was a joke, it should have ended there."

"But this young lady sent a second after that. You should have at least shown the courtesy of answering the first one. That is department policy, you know."

He knew. He had no real excuse to tell Avon. "I know I should have, but I didn't think she was for real. I could count on one finger the number of other inquiries like that I've received. Her second letter caught my attention, I must admit. I grew excited for a minute while I was listening to the files she sent. But the way things had been going, I didn't want to build up my hopes."

"What do you plan to do now you know she's real and her inquiry is an honest one?"

"What would I like to do or what should I do? I'd like to go after this and follow up on her work."

A sudden vibration shook the building. The tremor lasted for nearly a minute, jiggling the shelves until some of the books fell off. A loud crash came from the hallway, followed by the commotion of students rushing from the classrooms.

Greenefield looked at Troy and said, "That's the third one I've felt in the past week. I've lived in Kansas all my life and never felt them before."

"Something strange is going on here," Troy added. He helped her reshelf the fallen books. The noise in the hallway vanished back into the classrooms. They sat down in their respective chairs.

"Now, where were we?" Greenefield asked, speaking more to herself than to Troy. "Oh yes, your situation."

He shifted uncomfortably in his chair, feeling like a school boy taken into the assistant principal's office.

"My situation," he echoed.

"You're in a difficult position, Dr. Broadspeare."

DOCTOR Broadspeare. She hadn't called him that since the day they first met and the formalities of academia kept them distant until their friendship could blossom. Now the formality had returned.

"Dr. Broadspeare . . . Troy. Some on the tenure committee would like to see you gone. That's the brunt of it. The one factor that has kept you here has been your rapport with the students. But if the complaints of some of the students have borne the truth, I possibly should start wondering that as well."

"It was only that one time, I assure you," he said, his voice quavering in uncertainty. That had been the worst, the most egregious, but not the only time. It had happened more often than he wanted to admit, even to himself.

"You've been an excellent instructor, and your earlier work has brought a level of prestige to the department as well as the university. I, for one, have come to value your friendship. I would hate to lose you, but . . ." She broke eye contact and fingered the folder on the desk.

"But what? There's always a 'but' isn't there? Three little letters, three little very heavy letters."

"You needn't sound so hopeless. When one door closes, a window often opens." She picked up the folder with Welsey's information. Troy was thankful that she didn't include God in the cliché.

She continued. "This young lady may be the key to your future."

"Or it may be a wild goose chase. From everything you've been saying, I don't have many choices, do I?"

"No, you don't. The one thing I can offer you is a short-term research position. Consider it a type of sabbatical, but with a smaller stipend instead of your regular salary."

"My salary's not all that much to begin with, and I feel that you're pushing me against the wall."

"There is something else, and maybe this will make the bitter pill go down a bit easier." She stood up, reached across the top of her desk, and picked up a manila interoffice envelop. "I was going to send this through campus mail. I received it early this week and held on to it knowing we were going to meet."

"It's about the grant I wrote a while back, isn't it?"

She nodded giving a smiling "um-hum" behind the nod.

"And you held on to it all the same. But then if I get canned . . ."

"Now, Troy, nobody said anything about getting canned."

"Well, let's say, "let go." It's all the same. You held that back to get me to go along with your proposal, didn't you?

She continued to smile and gave a tilt of her head. If he didn't know better, he would have thought that she was flirting with him, or at least toying with him.

"I believe this is what you were hoping for." She handed him the envelope. With the eagerness of a child with a present, Troy took out his pocket knife and ran the blade under the flap and pulled out the pages.

It was all there—the full amount for the building of his subsonic lithographometer. He could finally have it built. He had been working on the design for several years and had all but given up on the notion that the money for it would ever come through.

"I read through it, but all the technical information confused me. Too much for this old woman."

"You're not that old," he said. "I'm not surprised you were confused. I picked up some of the ideas from Keene and modified them, making them more up to date using micro circuitry and . . ."

"Stop with the geek talk, Troy. Just tell me what it does."

"It's for listening to the ground. Not the earth under our shoes but the substrata rocks. That's where the deep vibrations come from. Those are the vibrations languages grow from. Just imagine it. With this, you can trace the history of languages, even ancient and lost ones back through the ones being spoken in that particular area. Not only the history, but recreate them—languages that haven't been spoken for centuries, or longer. Think of all the mysteries that have confounded us for so long that could be solved. At least that's the theory. Welsey, whether she knows it or not, may be noticing and ancient language trying to rise again through the stones."

"Listen to you go on. You haven't sounded this excited in a long time. Not since your wife left you."

"You want me to take this opportunity, don't you?"

"For the sake of your career, yes. And for the sake of you own well-being. If you don't take it, you'll more than likely lose your position at the university."

"And if I do take it, I may lose Sarah."

"Oh?"

Troy related to her what had been going on with their relationship, leaving nothing out, despite the strong possibility that he would offend Greenefield's Christianity.

Greenefield listened and he knew she was paying close attention to every word he said. Not only listened but cared. Only after he had finished, truly finished, did she speak. "As a woman, I believe I can speak for her. She wants what many women want, and that is a greater sense of security than the one she has with you. She is now finding part of that in the church group she had been led to. I know you are uncomfortable with my faith, and you also know that out of friendship and professional courtesy, I refrain from making a big deal over it. From the point of faith, I could say that the Lord has led her to where she now is. From that position, I could urge you to follow what she says, do the right thing by her, which means marrying her and settling down."

Troy squirmed even more knowing that from both the church and Sarah's positions, it is what he should do. After the last evening with Sarah, with her reaching out and caring for him. For nurturing—that was the word he had been searching for—nurturing him in a way that he had never received before, that had been alien to him, not receiving it from his mother. A caring that neither he nor his sister had received it from her as she became more and more wrapped up in her own world, a world that would finally destroy her. Only when Sarah nurtured him did discover how good it felt and how he could remain in it.

"You said from one position."

"Yes, from one position. The other is the one we talked of a few minutes ago. You need to revive your academic career. Your place here at the university is hanging by the barest thread. It is only that I promised the academic dean and others that you could revive it. I want you to read what she wrote for your file." She handed him the unopened folder. "It's good that that you are meeting with me and not the academic dean for an exit interview."

"I'll say one thing for you, Avon, you've always been completely honest with me, even when it hurts."

"Should you decide to leave, know that I would write a positive letter of recommendation should you look for some other position."

"Thanks." When he stood up to go, she also rose.

"One last question, Troy, and you don't have to answer it."

"What's that?"

"What do you love more?"

Her question wedged in like a thorn in the side. He returned to his office, closed the door, left the fluorescent light on, and plunked into his chair. The glare of the light bit into the books on the shelves. The white cinder-blocks grew cold, like the inside of the refrigerator. No wonder he preferred the darker light of the desk lamp that left the harsh corners of the room in the shadows. Too much light brings reality to the surface, and it was reality that Troy needed to face with no handy sort of tool like the Gobbledygook Generator to pull him out of it. He packed his briefcase with the copies of the files Avon had given him and left the building.

A cold wind from the north carried a gray sagging sky. Snow would be coming soon, and he hadn't had the car winterized yet. He often made mental notes to remind himself to get the common chores like car maintenance taken care of, then quickly forgot them so that each chore became an emergency, and each time he made the promise to do better next time, only to repeat the cycle time and time again. He got into the car and the engine cranked once and stopped. He turned off the ignition and tried again. A half-hearted sputter. He swore at the car, wishing he had bought a better one when he had the chance with his mother's inheritance instead of buying space in that vanity journal. It would have been a better way to spend the money. The journal backfired any way.

"Oh, please, please, God in heaven, let the car start," he said aloud. He paused as if giving the ritual prayer time to work, not that he believed in it. This time the engine caught and roared to life. On the drive home he was so distracted by Greenefield's final question that he ran a stop sign and clipped the end of new BMW.

"What the hell are you doing?" said the driver after he jumped out of the BMW. When the driver pulled himself to his full height, Troy hoped that it wouldn't come to a fight but would end with a quick exchange of insurance information because the driver filled in his tailored suit the way a retired NFL player would, a player who kept in shape, had used his NFL money wisely. The BMW driver crossed to the back of his car in three long strides, examined the damage, glanced at Troy's car and said, "Man, you better have a good insurance company, that's all I can say."

Before Troy could answer, the driver reached under his suit coat. Troy backed off, his eyes opening wide. He stumbled back against his car door, accidentally slamming it shut. The driver feinted a jump towards Troy and Troy leapt back, tripping over his feet and stumbling onto the pavement. The driver scowled down at Troy and started to laugh.

"Shit, this isn't anything but a cellphone." He pulled the phone from his jacket. "You think I'd be dumb enough to shoot you over a scratch like this? If I was white, I bet you wouldn't' be acting this way. I'm just calling the police to get this accident reported and let the blame fall on the right man."

While Troy got up off the ground and dusted off the road dirt, he overheard the driver make a second call. "Marge, Dimitri. I've had a little accident. Some dumbshit driver ran a stop sign and clipped my new car. Now listen, I need you to call Shovels and Barrows to tell them that I've been delayed. If they start getting huffy on you, remind them that they're the ones making a profit off me this time. And a damned good one at that. And Marge, you haven't heard anything from my daughter, have you? Damn. I'll see you when I get back."

The wail of the cruiser's siren grabbed their attention. The officer got out, looked at the damaged cars and then the men. He told them to get their registration forms and driver's licenses while he took notes of the accident. "Who's fault?"

"Mine, Officer," said Troy. He handed over his information to the officer.

"What'd ya do? Run a stop sign? I'll have to give you a citation." He glared at Troy when he handed back his registration and license. "You're damned lucky you only clipped the other car. You could have killed somebody."

For the second time of the day, Troy felt like he was in front of the assistant principal's desk. All he wanted to do now was go home but the officer told him to wait.

The officer read the other driver's information off the license. "Blevins, Dimitri. Say, you wouldn't happen to be the same Dimitri Blevins that played for the Chiefs, would you?"

Blevins nodded and said, "I'm surprised you'd remember. That was a long time ago."

"My dad used to take me to see you play. You wouldn't mind signing an autograph for him, would you?"

"It's been a long time since anybody's asked for my autograph. Be glad to."

"What have you been doing since you retired?"

"What's your dad's name?" He took the name, included it in the inscription, and handed it to the officer. "I do a little business in real estate and such over across the river from St. Louis. Keeps me busy."

"Thanks, Mr. Blevins." The officer pivoted and stared at Troy. "And you, I've got something for you to sign."

Troy signed the citation, thinking about the fine and the increase in the insurance rates. He also wondered how he could repair the car since he only carried liability because the value was so low. Before the officer left, he told him he had to get the headlight fixed or risk getting another ticket.

He tried to put the accident out of his mind by hoping that this homecoming would be a repeat of the last one. Of all the days, this is one where a quiet night with a beer poured and waiting along with a ready meal set in the scene of domestic tranquility would be enough to drive the answer to Greenefield's question.

When he got home, he found the house empty and a note left on the refrigerator. "Sorry I can't be home to greet you like last night. I forgot to tell you that I've joined the church's choir and practice is tonight. I didn't have chance to make anything, sorry. Maybe you could get a pizza or that Chinese carry-out you like so much."

Pizza, or Chinese, or anything else his heart desired and at this moment, it desired beer. He tossed the briefcase into the kitchen corner, grabbed a beer and drank, wishing it were stronger. He carried it with him when he went upstairs to change, and it was gone. By the time he had changed clothes he was ready for the second one. He descended the stairs with the eyes of his mind fixed on the next beer, and behind that one, a third and possibly fourth. Hunger hit after the second and he could care less what he ate. The combination of the risk of driving with a damaged headlight and the tipsiness tickling his brain, he had sense enough to stay home and scrounge through the kitchen. He came up with a large can of soup, stale crackers and string cheese.

He stumbled through the meal with half-hearted toasts to domestic tranquility. Leaving the dirty dishes on the table, he grabbed the briefcase and the next beer, greedily going after the contents of each.

He skipped the academic dean's report, not wanting to review its depressing contents. Far more important was the information Greenefield had turned up about Welsey, about Cahokia, and the grant for the lithographometer. The heart of the lithographometer lay within the intersection of linguistics, acoustics, and geology. He never believed he would ever get the funding for it, recalling the great difficulty Dr. Keene had in funding his research, and if not for the now defunct Corps of Extraordinary Phenomena, his work would have ground to a halt. With the corps' funding, Keene had begun creating his vibrational map of world's dialects using his trained ear and tuning forks. Troy wanted to make the study less dependent on the ears of a few, with their subjective leanings, and set the study of litholinguistics on solid, empirical ground. His device, with its integrated technology, would provide an aggressive step in that direction. With this opportunity, he could vindicate his old professor's work as well as his own career. Thanks to Avon Greenefield, he possibly would have the last laugh.

With a smile of satisfaction on his tipsy face, he examined the rest of the files. Both the one on Cahokia and the one on Welsey were more complete than those he had. Undoubtedly, they were the work of one of Avon's graduate assistants and, in the effort to remain in her good graces, were both thorough and professional. In the report he found the name of one of his father's former students, Alan Gide. Troy vaguely remembered him because he was in the seventh grade when Gide worked with his father. As Troy recalled, he was typical of his father's students, tall, thin, earnest, and eager to be out in the field to spend long hours brushing away bits of dust and debris from some bare spot of earth in hopes of overturning some artifact, some scrap of ancient culture that meant little to the original owner but invaluable in modern archeological circles. Then Troy remembered that Gide had taught him to throw and catch a football, something his father never had the time or ability to do.

Gide had led the dig into Mount 72 of Cahokia that had uncovered the human sacrifices which had taken place in the ancient city. He was also the lead scientist fighting for greater preservation of the site against the encroachment of developers like Dimitri Blevins of Blevins Holdings. That was a name Troy never wanted to come across again and the mention of it brought back the memory of the accident, sending him for another beer, as if that could bring on amnesia.

After half the bottle was gone, he turned Welsey Yergen's file. Impressive, he thought, when he saw that her first published essay had been written when she was still an undergraduate on the migration of Aztec writing styles. Her graduate work had been more accomplished, looking good until he matched up the dates. All of her work was at least seven years old, seven years between her public record of graduate work and now. But why, he wondered, had she called herself a graduate student when no record of her being in a graduate program existed. She should have finished by now. She should have completed her doctorate and published her dissertation. She should be teaching somewhere, but he couldn't find any evidence for it. He reread the file, thinking that in his confused tipsiness he might have missed something. The rereading confused the issue further because as he looked at her transcripts, he saw that she hadn't finished her master's degree, and was only three hours short. By the time he finished the fifth beer he began talking out loud.

"Welsey, what happened to you, young lady?"

He picked up her photo from the file, an 8x10 that was an improvement over the Facebook picture he had seen. He moved it to better light. Deep brown eyes set against soft brown skin looked out at him. Her finely sculpted nose contrasted with the gentle kinkiness of her hair. He carried the photo into the living room, talking to it as if she could hear him. "You only had one class to complete. Only one class. What did you do? Run out of money? I hope you didn't do something foolish like get pregnant and have to drop out before you finished. I've known too many who have walked that path, Miss Yergens. It always broke my heart to see it. You had so much promise? What happened? And why did you call yourself a graduate student when you no longer are?"

He lay down on the couch and the room began to spin. "Welsey, I think I drank too much. I'm going to take a nap." He fell asleep with her photo in his hand.

Chapter 3

"Honey. Troy, Honey." He woke with tension choking his neck. Sarah stood over him, holding the empty bottle in one hand and Welsey's photo in the other.

"I must have fallen asleep."

"What happened? I found four empty bottles in the kitchen, a pan still on the burner with the soup burnt dry, and you in here with this." She held up the photo.

"You're not going to believe what happened to me today. Sit down, Sarah. I don't think you're going to like what I have to say."

"Is it her?"

"Her?" He looked at the photo she had waved in front of his eyes. "I've never met her. That's the girl who emailed me about Cahokia. I've decided to go there. I have to. It's either that or lose my job."

"And what would be wrong with that? All you've been doing for the past year is complaining about the poor quality of the students, the mindless committee work, the uselessness of your research. This could be the chance for us to start a new life together. A position is about to open up at the library. . ."

Troy stood up without hearing the rest of the sentence. He knew the answer to Greenefield's last question despite the drunkenness. He knew the answer and he reached for Welsey's photo. "Give me the picture," he demanded.

A sudden tremor rattled the house, knocking books off the shelves and them off their feet.

"This is what I'm talking about," Troy said. "The earthquakes. They're trying to tell us something and she is onto a part of the puzzle." He pointed to the photo Sarah continued to clutch in her hand.

"Are you crazy? The earthquakes are telling us something. You're saying the earthquakes are talking?"

"In a way, yes. The vibrations of the ground coming from the substrata of bedrock influence our speech. This is what I've given most of my academic life to prove."

"I thought you put all that behind you. I thought that you and I could become a proper family instead of . . ." She looked at the photo, then Troy, and released the photo that fluttered to the floor.

"Instead of what?" his voice softened and he sheltered her elbow in the hollow of her hand.

"Instead of a slut."

"I never thought of you that way." He reached out with his other hand to embrace her. She brushed him away.

"It doesn't matter what you thought. It's what I thought, and what I've been led to think."

"It's your church friends who put this into your head. Ever since you started chumming around with them, our lives have been different. You moved into the guestroom when I needed you the most."

"Needed me? For what, a bed partner?"

"The last six months have been a nightmare. I needed you to believe in me, and you weren't there. And now I have the chance to regain faith in myself and the work I do, and I find us arguing."

"Troy, don't you see that I have needs as well? I moved into the guestroom because I didn't feel right sleeping with you anymore. It wasn't because of my church friends, as you call them. The feeling came before. I thought if I stayed and showed you a different sort of relationship, we could become a family, a real family."

"Family? I've been down that road before and look what happened."

Sarah moved to the doorway. "I'm not her, Troy Broadspeare. I never was, but now I can see why she left you. We don't matter to you. Not your friends, not your family, not your students. The only thing at matters to you is that crazy---and it is nuts—crazy idea of rocks talking. I used to think you made that up to get a cozy teaching job."

Troy, woozy from the beer, lunged towards her, grabbed her shoulders, and pushed her out of the doorway.

"You need to go." He looked into her eyes and saw the chill rising from them, the accusations, the righteous condemnation. "You need to go tonight before I regret something I'll regret later."

He lurched past her, stumbled up the stairs, and into the guestroom.

"What are you doing in there?" he heard her say as she ran up the stairs.

"Packing. Packing your things." He opened the closet and threw the clothes on the bed, followed by the contents of the dresser drawers that he dumped on top.

"Stop it. Stop it. You're out of your mind. I'm going, look, I'm going." She grabbed the handful of clothes off the bed and clutched them tightly. She held onto the clothes with one hand while reaching for the cell phone with the other.

"I'm going, Troy, I'm going. Just let me call Betty. I should be able to stay with her."

The news that Betty would take in Sarah calmed the blood pounding in Troy's head. He stood by, watching her pack as much as she could in the three suitcases that first brought her clothes into his house. More had been accumulated over the four years they had been together, many that he had bought her. Before she had finished, Betty's car pulled into the driveway. Betty gave a short signal with the horn and Sarah's cell rang.

"I'm fine, Betty. He's calmer now. I don't think he'd mind if you came in and gave a hand." She pleaded for permission with her eyes. Troy nodded and stepped into the hallway.

"Tell her to come on in if she wants to."

The front door open and Betty called out.

"Come on up, if you want to."

She marched past him, keeping careful distance. The stare she gave him was filled with accusation and condemnation. He wondered if she would later grill Sarah about all the abuse she must have been suffering at the hands of this monster disguised as a mild college professor. She had done this before, Troy realized. He felt categorized and wrongly labeled for up until that night, he had never done anything that could remotely be called abuse. Neglect during finals and grading, maybe, but not abuse, not verbal, emotional, or physical.

Betty carried one suitcase to Sarah's two as they made their way down the stairs.

"Sarah," Troy said, not sure why he called her name.

"Don't stop, Sarah," Betty said, urging her on. "Don't look at him. That's what they want. Don't do it. Follow me straight out to the car."

Troy followed them down the stairs, keeping several steps between them. He would have opened the door, but Betty beat him to it. It was like she was following a script.

"Get in the car. Get in as quickly as you can. I'll get the door." She slammed the front door shut, leaving Troy inside. The engine roared to life and the tires gave a sharp squeal when the car pulled out and sped out of the subdivision.

The beer had worn off, leaving Troy exhausted. In the living room Welsey's photo lay face down where it had fallen. He picked it up and set it on the bookcase and addressed it. "I don't know what you've gotten me into, Welsey Yergens, but we're in for it now."

The rest of the semester passed quickly. The immediate improvement of the students surprised Troy. He managed to talk Thrace into reconsidering his major. Word quickly spread that Sarah was out of his life and he would be taking a sabbatical the next semester. A few rumors circulated that this sabbatical included a do or die project. The rumor mill kicked into high gear when the ad came out announcing the auctioning off of his furniture and putting the house on the market. He realized that if he didn't succeed in Cahokia, he wouldn't be coming back. And if he did succeed, he had no need of a house. All an empty house did for him before was get him in with Sarah. Part of his desire for her was to share the house so he wouldn't feel lonely in the evenings. Now a small apartment would serve as well.

Work on the lithographometer went well after he found a fabricator who could follow his specialized instructions. The builder had dropped out of college, lived in his mother's basement, and surrounded himself with electronics and surveillance equipment. "Most of my work I can't tell you about. That's why I can't give you any references, but I can do the work. Your specs aren't that special. The only weird thing is the frequencies you want it tuned for. They seem too low to do much good. Not even the Navy's ELF goes this low. And the way you want them amped up... If you're not careful, you're going to blow out your eardrums, or maybe your brains. I did one upgrade you didn't call for, a touch-screen. Check it out."

Troy turned on the machine and an oscilloscope filled the screen. He turned one of the dials and the screen came to life, tracking every ambient noise in the basement.

"You can use the screen to fine tune it."

Troy touched the screen with one finger and pushed the frequencies to higher levels.

"Pretty cool, isn't it? It'll only cost you and extra two-hundred bucks," said the fabricator.

"Two hundred? That's not what we agreed on earlier," Troy complained.

"Two hundred for the upgrade. Take it or leave it."

Troy knew he had no choice. He paid the man and took his machine.

Finals week caught Troy in a swirl of activities beyond the swarm of essays and exams that had to be taken care of. The auction had taken most of his household goods away. The sale of the house sent him packing the few things he kept in the local U-Store warehouse. He had enough room left over in the cubicle so that he could have set up a cot and lived there, but he took a room at an extended stay hotel.

Throughout this, he had been in contact with Welsey, telling her that he had received his sabbatical, that he had a new device to help them, and that he would be on his way shortly after the end of the fall semester. She responded first with excitement, but then her emails grew wary. She asked if they could delay their meeting until after the first of the year, given the excuse of Christmas being family time. The last comment pushed him to the think of Sarah. He hadn't thought much about her since the night she left with Betty. Christmas time in his family hadn't been all that different from other times, except that his father's teaching load lessened. His brother Anixameter was still in Greece and Athena, his sister, was in Brussels with her family. Money was too tight to afford a flight to either one. While Avon had made the polite offer that he spend Christmas her and her family, he refused with equal politeness, to the relief of both of them.

"What are you going to do then, Troy? Not sit in that hotel room by yourself, are you?" she asked at their final meeting before his sabbatical.

"No, I'm going to take a slow drive across Missouri. I've never done that before. I've always been in a hurry to get from one place to the other. I found quite a few caves between here and Cahokia. I've been thinking of trying out the lithographometer in some of them. Maybe take my time and stop at whatever else might strike my fancy. I'm not meeting with Welsey until the January 4th."

She walked him to the exit out of the building. "You know that I would pray a blessing on you if you would accept it."

"And if I was a believer, I'd accept it."

"I'll give you a hug instead." In their embrace, she slipped a motherly kiss on his cheek. He went out the door and crossed the parking lot to his car, knowing that behind the closed door, Dr. Avon Greenefield had her head bowed and hands clasped in prayer.

His first destination was a show cave whose billboard advertisements lined the interstates throughout the Missouri River Valley. The closer he got, the more signs promising a Jeweled Cavern, Secret Lakes, Largest Stalagmite, and all the other allurements tourists could desire. Troy chose it because it was convenient and a safe place to test the lithographometer. When he pulled into the parking lot, he saw more people leaving than entering. The glum faces of the children matched the scowls of the parents. Approaching the gift shop that also served as the cave's entrance, he saw the reason why—a sign announcing, "Cave closed due to earthquake threat. Gift Shop Open."

In the hopes that he could convince the operators to make an exception for him because he came as a professional researcher and not a tourist, he parked, and went into the gift shop. The shop carried an array of trinkets that children begged their parents for with the pleas of "I've got to have it," and "I won't ask for anything else, I promise." He strode by the racks of merchandise without a glance and found the person who looked to be in charge. She was a matronly looking woman in grey pants and tan blouse with a shoulder patch and name tag that mimicked Missouri's Department of State Parks.

Troy put on his best smile, introduced himself, and made his request. The way she examined his business card before folding it in half gave him the answer before she could open her mouth.

"But I'm not a tourist."

The wall of her expression didn't budge. "I'm sorry Dr. Broadstreet."

"It's Broadspeare, Ma'am."

"As I explained before, Dr. Broadspeare, we can't let anyone into the cave right now, not even the staff. The recent tremors have made it unsafe. We have heard some shifting going on down there, and we don't know what the conditions might be. No. The threat is too great."

There was no getting around her.

He glanced at the junk in the gift shop and left with disgust, not realizing he was being followed. He put his hand on the car door handle when he heard someone call out, "Dr. Broadstreet?"

He turned around to face the voice. It came from a short, wiry young man with a wisp of beard trying to cover his chin.

"The name's Broadspeare."

"Broadspeare. Got it. You're some kind of doctor who's looking for a cave?"

"I teach at Kansas Eastern." He kept his hand on the handle, anxious to get on the road. "And yes, I was hoping to find the cave open."

The young man ran his tongue over his teeth and pulled back his lips revealing dark and crooked teeth. "I got a cave. Or I know of one you could get into. A real nice one with all sorts of crystals and stalagmites and tunnels. It's on my uncle's farm. I might be able to persuade him to let you look at it." He leaned against the car with his arms folded over his chest.

"How much and how far way?"

"Tain't that far. A few miles down the road. And for the other, I'll have to find out. Give me a minute." He walked away from Troy, took out his phone, and called. From the distance, Troy couldn't overhear the conversation. The young man held the phone away from his ear, looked at Troy, and called out, "Fifty Dollars."

Fifty. The tourist cave would only have been ten and all he needed was fifteen minutes underground. "Tell him I'll give him ten."

"But that don't leave nothing for me mister, er, doctor."

"Fifteen then."

The young man went back to his cell, then called out again, "Thirty. He's come down to thirty."

"All right, make it thirty."

The young man relayed the message to his uncle and told him they would be at the cave entrance soon.

Troy agreed to follow the young man who took off in a rattling pick-up lacking a tailgate. The "soon" be became longer than he counted upon and the few miles must have been the way of the crow as Troy followed him around winding roads that began with asphalt, turned into gravel, then dirt, and finally a deeply rutted lane with a strip of overgrown weeds running down the middle. The lane came to an end at the bottom of a cliff that shot up out of the ground like a waiting missile. He pulled up next to the pick-up and got out. The burnt-out husk of a building stood next to the entrance to the cave. The cave opening was blocked with a heavy wooden door that hung precariously to the hinges that were driven into the stone. Sitting on a four-wheeler was a man who had to be the uncle, wearing a stained barn coat over his bib overalls that stretched across his great belly. He reached into this pocket and pulled out a fistful of keys.

"Jeb, catch." He tossed the keys to the young man. Jeb unlocked the padlock holding the chain that wove through the rotting boards of the door.

"I've gotta keep it locked to keep the damned kids out. Last thing I need is some son-of-a-bitch idiot falling down in there and bringing down a law suit on my head."

Jeb tugged and the door, dragging its bottom through the dirt and the weeds, opened it barely wide enough to let someone through. Troy took the case holding the lithographometer from the car, it's shiny aluminum reflecting bands of light from the afternoon sun onto the rock wall.

"You got the cash" asked the uncle. Troy took out a ten and a twenty and gave it to him. "Hey, Jeb, git over here and take yer share. And give me the keys while yer at it." He took the keys from Jeb and handed him the ten. He shifted his bulk in the four-wheeler's seat. The seat groaned in complaint. "You know, perfessor, I would have taken twenty-five. Twenty for me and five for Jeb." He laughed as his belly shook making the four-wheeler vibrate in reply. "Jeb, you stay and wait for him, then lock 'er up again. Got it?"

"Yes, Uncle Bubba."

Troy hadn't planned on spelunking alone in an undeveloped cave. With Dr. Keene he had explored caverns and tombs that many others had already visited and most of them had been equipped with lights for tourists. Fortunately, he had put new batteries in the flashlight that he carried in the glove box. He tested it, picked up the case, and headed into the cave.

The beam of light flashed on remnants of bottles and cans left over from parties of years ago. No one had brewed Drewery's beer since his father was young. Deeper into the cave, the human debris gave way to animal and then nothing. The floor was dry and even, like the bottom of an old stream. The light from the entrance grew smaller and smaller until it looked the size the one Alice used to enter the Red Queen's domain. He had gone far enough. He found a rock shelf the right size and height for the lithographometer. He set the case down, opened it, and turned it on. The LEDS came to life, giving enough light so that he could turn off the flash light and set it down. He made the first adjustment, congratulating himself over the success of his design. The fabricator had done an excellent job. He tuned the frequencies. The scope moved in slow, undulating cycles that matched the drawl of Jeb and his uncle's speech. He put on the headphones and listened to the rising and falling of the tones. The changes in tone grew into a rhythmic pulse, and an ancient beat growing from deep in the earth. His body caught it and he swayed ever so slightly back and forth. He had never felt this before and the feeling was one of wonderment. He broke the reverie and spoke to the machine with a voice echoing what he had heard and it sounded like Jeb saying, "Ya done good, boy. Ya done good."

Suddenly the machine screamed in a high-pitched tone and Troy jerked the headphones form his head. The oscillator went wild and he heard a rumble from deep within the cave. The ground pitched from under his feet and he fell backwards, striking his head against the rock wall and knocking him out. When he came to, utter darkness surrounded him. He must have closed the case when he fell. He reached around for the flashlight. He nudged it with his fingertips and then heard it fall, clattering in the darkness, A hole hadn't been there before, he remembered. He stretched out on the ground, edging towards where the flash light had been. He gripped the sharp edges of a drop off made sharp from having been sheared off.

The cell phone! He pulled it out and turned it on. In the intense darkness, its dull glow filled the cave with an eerie light. The lithographometer had fallen from its shelf, but it seemed to be intact. He realized the piercing shriek he heard was the scream of the rocks grinding through an earthquake, a slight tremor that rattled a few knick-knacks, but little more. He started up the path he had come down, expecting to see the small doorway of light ahead. It wasn't there. Maybe I haven't gone far enough. He continued and discovered he couldn't see the light. The tremor that opened the ground at one end of his path had sent a boulder down the other end. He groped around and found a small opening on the left side of it, barely wide enough to squeeze through.

He picked up a pebble and tossed it through the opening and listened. No sound came back. "Well, Troy, that could mean a deep hole, or it fell on sand and didn't make any noise, or anything else. What are you going to do?" He knew what he had to do. He couldn't wait for help. Other than Jeb and his uncle, nobody knew he was here. His meeting with Welsey was more than three weeks into the future. "And I doubt if those two are going to tell the sheriff to send out a search party. They'll probably strip the car, sell it for parts, and then good-bye to Dr. Troy Broadspeare."

He thrust his hand through the opening and felt a way through the opening. Inch by inch he crawled, keeping the lithographometer with him, pushing it ahead, or clutching it to his chest, and once, looping his foot through the handle and dragging. The rocks scratched his hands and tore his clothes. Once, he lifted his head and cracked his skull. Warm blood dropped down his face and he wiped it from his eyes with the back of his hand. Finally, he saw the pin-prick of light of the opening. He found the path. Stretching to his full height, he strode up the path with the cell phone lighting the path.

Jeb sat where Troy had left him. "Dam, what the hell happened to you, doc? Looks like you fell down a hole in the ground." He laughed at his joke.

"You could say something like that."

"You know, doc, I think we had an earthquake. It was weird. The birds all of a sudden shut up and the ground gave a little shake lie this." He took Troy by the shoulders and gave him a quick shake.

"Is that all it was?"

"Not much more than that. Now that you're out, I can lock it up. Uncle Bubba can be mean if you don't do exactly what he says. Come back any time, doc."

The damage to his body looked worse than it was. The crack on the skull left a small scratch and the aches left as he soaked in the tub at the Motel 8 in Hermann, Missouri. He stopped in Hermann because the car's temperature gauge kept spiking after an hour on the road. The motel's clerk recommended a mechanic, Claude Chambers, "the best in town." The car could wait until morning. He had to take care of his body first and the long soak did it a world of good. After he rose from the tub, he closed the curtains against the late December sky and went to bed.

He looked at the alarm clock that said "9" and he believed he had taken a long nap, only to be surprised at the strong light shining through the crack in the window, a light declaring that morning had arrived. The rigors of yesterday's spelunking gave fresh pains to his muscles. He knew the stiffness would loosen up after several days.

He phoned the mechanic who told him that he could look at his car but made no promises as to when he could finish the job, nor would he give an estimate over the phone. The mechanic's shop lay in downtown Hermann, a former gas station that had long ceased to pump gas and now provided a living for the mechanic and a part-time helper. It was a short drive to the garage, but the temperature had spiked again. When he pulled in, steam rolled out from under the hood.

"It's over heating," said the Claude.

"How could a car overheat in the middle of December?"

"Could be the thermostat. Could be a leak in one of the cooling lines. Could be a cracked gasket. Could be a lot of things."

Claude opened the hood and pulled out the oil dipstick. "Oil looks good, other than needing a change. That rules out the head gasket. I can't get to it now, like I told you on the phone, but if you leave your keys, I'll get to it as soon as I can. I'll need a number where I can reach you."

Troy gave him one of his cards with everything crossed out except the cell number. Troy handed it to him and said, "You're not from around her are you, even though most people think you've been here forever."

Claude took the card, cocked his head, and asked, "How'd you know that? You some kind of detective?"

"I'm not a detective. Your accent gave you away. Buried under your Missouri drawl is a trace of Minnesota. Northern Minnesota."

"Well, I'll be switched. You're right. I was born in Minnesota close to the Canadian border and we moved here when I was three. My dad took a call to pastor the Lutheran church here in town. That's more than 60 years ago. You need a ride back to the motel?"

Troy declined the ride saying that the walk would do him good.

Hermann, Missouri, caught the prosperous flow of the nation's renewed interest in local wineries. The town had been founded by Germans from the Rhineland who brought their viniculture along with their religion and language. "Before Prohibition," the pamphlet that Broadspeare had picked up from the visitor's center informed him, "Hermann had been known as the Rhineland of Missouri." The town was working to regain that spirit with several wineries adding restaurants and shops with a façade of German quaint. Troy walked through the town, taking in a town ready to celebrate Christmas and decked out in it holiday finery. The buzz of his phone interrupted his window shopping.

"Mr. Broadspeare, This is Claude down at the shop. I've got news about your car."

"Do I need to sit down?" He saw the public bench in front of a candy store and sat down.

"No, I don't think so, but it depends. The good news is that only two things are wrong with it, and the parts are cheap, if I can get 'em."

"What does that mean?"

"This car's got some years on it. I can get a thermostat, no problem. It that was all it was, I'd have you on the road in less than an hour."

"And the other?" Troy gripped the edge of the bench.

"The other is the cooling lines. The radiator's fine, but the rail that runs along the back has got a couple of holes in it. This is normally a dealer part. I checked with the Ford dealer in town and he ain't got one. He said he'd have to order it and it might take up to a week."

"A week! I don't have a week. I need to be in East St. Louis."

"Now hold on, Mr. Broadspeare. I've got a friend who might be able to help. He's retired, and I should be able to convince him to patch it up for you. He's an old radiator man from way back."

"Do you think he could do it?"

"I already talked to him and I convinced him that you seemed like a nice enough feller and he agreed to. It'll cost less than a new part anyways."

"How soon can he get to it?"

"Not till after Christmas. He's got to visit his grandkids. We should have you on the road again by the twenty-seventh, twenty-eighth at the latest."

Troy sighed. It must have been loud enough for Claude to hear.

"You all right, Mr. Broadspeare?"

"Yes, I'm fine."

"I hope you don't think I'm out of line by saying this, but what are you doing for Christmas?"

"I haven't thought about it."

"Well, it don't seem right that somebody has to spend Christmas alone in a motel. If you don't mind my asking, Mr. Broadspeare, I'd like to invite you to join me and my family at the Christmas Eve service at church."

"I'm not a very religious man, Mr. Chambers."

"Call me Claude. And it don't matter if you're religious or not. My granddaughter's leading the choir and the music if beautiful. You like music, don't ya?"

"Yes, but I was planning . . ."

"Then come for that. I'll be by to pick you up at the motel around seven. I guarantee you won't regret it."

Claude pulled up to the portico of the motel at exactly seven. When Troy got into the immaculate 1954 Ford F-100 pick-up he had to comment on its condition.

"She's my baby, a restoration project. She needed to get her weekly drive, so I figured I might as well show her off to you. I'm still working on the heater, so there's a blanket if you need it." He pointed to the folded afghan on the seat.

"Why are you doing this, Mr. Chambers?

"Claude, if you don't mind. You come across as a nice, intelligent guy, maybe a bit lonely around the edges. And I figured an educated man like you would enjoy the music if nothing else. By the way," Claude took out a small piece of paper from his pocket and handed it to him. "Here's your ticket to get in."

"A ticket? Since when does anyone need a ticket to get into a church?"

"Like I said, tonight's a special service. Half the town will be there. If we sold the tickets, we'd make a mint, but they're only for crowd control." He pulled into the parking lot of St. Mark's Lutheran Church and searched for an empty space. "Maybe I should have picked you up earlier. I don't want to park her out in the street." He pulled into the last parking place in the back row, farthest from the church. Clusters of people—families, extended families, and couples. A group that appeared to have been waiting on the steps waved at Claude and Troy.

"That's my wife," said Claude as he returned her wave. "We'd best hurry."

Claude's wife was plump in a way that befitted her station in life. "You must be the one Claude told me about." She extended her hand to Troy. He took it, surprised at the strength of the grip beneath the pudginess of flesh. The music of the organ drifted out of the church at the opening of the door. A tall, sturdy man dressed in a Beefeater's costume opened the door while another, equally sturdy Beefeater took the tickets and clicked off a counter as they went in. Troy asked the reason for the costumes.

"Didn't Claude tell you that this is our annual Boar's Head Festival?" she replied.

"He told me it was a Christmas Eve service."

She glared at her husband. Claude shrugged it off with "Service, festival, what's the difference? It's still church."

They entered and when Troy heard the first notes of the orchestra tuning up, he turned to look into the balcony that was filled to overflowing with the choir and orchestra, including tympanum. He scanned the bulletin and discovered that this was a combined service with thanks being given to the other churches and the Orchestra of Westminster College. He also saw that Ragan Chambers directed the program. He elbowed Claude and pointed to her name. The broad grin on the mechanic's face gave an answer filled with pride.

The secular gave way to the sacred after the boar's head was paraded through on the shoulders of the Beefeaters with the Wise Men following close behind. The rest of the Christmas story followed. Within the it, the church wove a regular liturgical service. Troy fidgeted for a moment, feeling like he had when he was eleven and his grandmother had forced him to go to church. He felt that Claude had suckered him into this and the resentment clenched the muscles in his neck to block his ears. He didn't want to hear this or be part of it. He wasn't about to join in the chanting of the psalm, echoing back to the pastor the verses in response. Those surrounding him might, but not him. Wedged into the pews the way they were, he felt the vibrations of their bodies as they sang; the rhythm going back and forth, a slow, low rhythm that he caught. He had felt this before, and not that long ago. The memory felt fresh, but where? The psalm stopped, and the service went on. Troy would have fallen asleep if not for the gentle nudge from Claude.

"Are you sure I can't get to you come over for Christmas Dinner tomorrow?" asked Claude when he dropped Troy off at the motel.

"I'm sure," he said and assured him that he would be all right, adding that he didn't mind being alone. Troy needed to be alone so that he could try to remember where he had had that feeling before. The issue nagged at him, got under his skin, and was working its way into the muscles, muscles that still

70

ached from that crawl in the cave. He fell asleep with the question on his mind, tossing and turning through the night.

He woke up tired. He fiddled with the TV and found nothing of interest. Seventy channels and nothing. No wonder he never bothered getting cable for himself. He left the motel and saw how right Claude had been. At least the motel had internet, which he used to email Welsey to tell her of the delay, that he would be arriving by ferry in Modoc, and that she should meet him there.

The streets of Hermann were empty except for the snow that had drifted down, covering the few tracks made on the road and sidewalk. As he walked past one closed restaurant after another, he wished he hadn't been so adamant about refusing Claude's offer. He began to feel homeless, walking the streets, and looking into empty parking lots. The line of cars parked at the strip mall on the far edge of town gave him hope, as did the aroma of spice that came from Hermann's lone Chinese restaurant. At least he could be fed.

He joined the rest of the disconnected and was seated by himself in a back booth. He ordered without thinking and ate without tasting. Christmas had never been all that special to him. Most of his childhood had been spent following his father's archeological diggings which were often in countries where open celebrations of Christmas were, if not forbidden, strongly discouraged. He could recall only two Christmas celebrations that fit the category of festival and both had been held at the American embassies. Once he had gone with Sarah to visit her parents, but since he was the cause of her moral downfall, his presence was tolerated more than welcomed. On his walk back to the motel, he found himself humming the tones of the psalm that had been sung the night before without knowing why, except that the familiarity remained undaunted and unexplained. He also came across an announcement for the annual Hermann wine fest. The iconic form of a German in lederhosen surrounded by blonde and buxom women proclaimed—"Dec. 26- 31. Special food, wine tasting, and dancing." Instead of the typical beer steins, wine glasses filled their hands.

"If the car's not done, this will give me something to do," he said to the empty street. The car wasn't finished, Claude told him, but the radiator was being repaired and should be done the next day.

The contrast between the twenty-fifth and twenty-sixth of December in downtown Hermann was sharpened by the weather for the snow had stopped and the temperature hovered in the mid-20s, calm, with a bright sun, the kind of weather that brings people out who have already tired of the cold grey that haunts November and December. The shops were open, and the clerks wore what their common Germanic memory considered traditional costumes. Attractive young women stood outside the restaurants with trays of samples. Gift shops set out tables of special sales. And since this was St. Stephen's Day, someone dressed as Good King Wenceslaus paraded through the town, greeting everyone, although most confused him with Father Christmas and he imported more than a tad of Bacchus about him with a crown of plastic vines and grapes circling his head.

Broadspeare wandered and mingled with the crowds, tasting samples and examining wares. Freely he tasted and freely he browsed until the music coming from one of the wine tasting rooms called him in.

Familiar voices mixed with the singing, and he had to find out the source.

The familiar voices came from Claude and his wife. Each held a glass of wine in one hand and a sheet of lyrics in the other, although they paid little attention to the words on the page, singing by heart. Broadspeare noticed that the mechanic stumbled for some of the words. Claude saw him, raised his glass, and motioned him over. Troy bought a commemorative glass that promised inexpensive refills throughout the festival, had it filled, and stood between Claude and his wife who handed him a song sheet. He found the song and joined in. When they finished, she looked up at him and smiled, "Why Mr. Broadspeare, you've a fine tenor voice. Did you sing in a choir? Our granddaughter would love to have you in her choir. She complains that she can't find many good tenors. Here she is now."

Ragan Chambers had been accompanying the singers on the tasting room's piano. She moved towards them with a grace that kept her from brushing up against anyone. To Troy, it looked like dancing, or a ballet, and she had the figure of a ballet dancer, if such dancers could be nearly six-feet tall.

"Ragan," said Claude's wife, "I've found a tenor for you. Mr. Broadspeare, this is Ragan, our granddaughter."

Ragan extended her hand for Tony to take. Her long fingers wrapped around his hand, the long fingers of a pianist.

"It's very nice to meet you, Mr. Broadspeare."

Troy paused before giving his reply. Her accent caught him off-guard. The Missouri drawl that he had been hearing throughout Hermann had barely taken root. "And it's very nice to meet you as well," he said, after recovering his composure. "I thoroughly enjoyed your program last night."

"Thank you." Her base accent carried notes from the East Coast.

"He's got a great tenor voice," chimed in Claude's wife.

"I'm sure he has, Gram, but I don't think he intends on staying here."

Claude stepped in, "Come on, dearie. It's getting late for us. Hammie said he'd have that part all done early in the morning and I want to get it in as soon as I can." Turning to Troy he added, "I'll call you at the motel as soon as it's done." He pulled his wife from the tasting room.

"You must have made a good impression," Ragan said.

"Why do you say that?"

"Gram's usually very protective of her favorite granddaughter."

He listened, without paying attention to her words, then said, "You're from the East Coast, Virginia and North Carolina."

"Did she tell you that?"

"No, you did. It's in your voice. You also trained overseas, in Eastern Europe."

"Mr. Broadspeare, what have you been doing, looking up my biography or something?"

"No. And it's Dr. Broadspeare. I'm a linguist and I pay attention to accents, that's all. I hope I haven't offended you."

"I'm not offended, but it is unnerving, *Doctor* Broadspeare."

"I'll make you a deal. If you call me Troy and let me buy you a glass of wine, I won't dissect your accent anymore."

"It's a deal, but you'll have to buy me that wine in another shop. I've been here all night and I need a breath of fresh air."

They grabbed their coats and carried their glasses out into the street. Good King Wenceslaus was now accompanied by two Rhine maidens who poured wine into any open glass that passed them by.

"I'm confused," said Troy, "For Christmas, there's Wenceslaus, who looks like Bacchus, accompanied by Wagnerian Rhine maidens. What kind of festival is this?"

"The kind that attracts tourists to the wineries in the off season. Let's go in here." She pointed to a shop down one of the side streets. "It's quieter, and the wine is better."

She was right on both counts. They sat down in a back corner where little of the light from the festival shone. She told him that his guesses about her were true. Her mother had left Hermann for college in Roanoke, Virginia, with the intention of becoming a Lutheran pastor but, "as Gram would say, 'found herself in a family way.' She was too ashamed to move back, so she raised me on the coast. And yes, I did study music in Belgrade."

"So how did you come to settle in Hermann?"

"We used to visit when I was a child and the place always felt right. When the vineyards took off and the town's culture began to change, I realized I wanted to be part of it. It doesn't make sense, does it?"

Following an outlandish dream made perfect sense to Troy. They left the shop after a second glass and strolled by the river on the newly constructed boardwalk. She took his arm and he enjoyed the warmth of her touch. "And what about you? What brings you to town?"

"An accident. The car broke down."

She leaned against him as they walked. "I'm not sure I believe in accidents."

He put his arm around her shoulders while they continued down the boardwalk. Why had he told her he was a linguist and not a litholinguist? Was he ashamed or did want to avoid going through the rigmarole of trying to explain his theories only to be met with a quizzical look, or worse, rolling eyes that mocked him. He'd been in these situations before and he didn't like it. He was tempted to stop walking, pull her to him and kiss her. Even through their thick winter coats, he could tell that she wouldn't mind, and might welcome it.

The snow began to fell in thick, heavy flakes.

"I suppose you'll have to leave tomorrow, won't you? If Gramps is finished with your car, that is."

"Yes. I'm doing research over in Illinois, just across the Mississippi near East St. Louis."

"I haven't heard anyone say anything good about East St. Louis is a long time."

"I'm not interested in the East St. Louis. I'm supposed to meet someone."

"Ah," she said with a knowing sigh. "I suppose if you have to leave, you have to leave. Thank you for the wine, Dr. Broadspeare. It's been a pleasant evening."

She left him on the boardwalk. The snow turned wet, mixing with freezing drizzle. He wondered why his feet seemed to freeze in place. He tried to form the words telling her to stop but his mouth went suddenly dry and his throat closed down. For an instant he imagined going after her and giving up this cockamamie venture. He could drop between the cracks of the boardwalk and stay in Hermann—there had to be at least an adjunct teaching job. He could leave his tattered reputation in the caves and live in Ragan's light. The drizzle turned to a cold rain, chilling his imagination. The walk to the hotel would be long and dismal.

Chapter 4

Claude's phone call woke him at eight and by nine Troy was headed toward Ste. Genevieve to take the ferry across the Mississippi.

One of the last remaining ferries ran between Ste. Genevieve and Modoc, Illinois. The five-car ferry made the run four times per day for those who would prefer to avoid going miles out of their way to catch either the bridge at St. Louis or Chester, Illinois. No major highways run east and west through the ports the ferry serves, if they can be called ports, more like places where the road ends and the ferry crossing began. Troy drove his Taurus wagon from Hermann to Ste. Genevieve through the mountains, taking his time. While the interstate would have been faster, they would not have provided the linguistic scenery need to tune his ear to the locale. Even though he could pick up nuances the majority of the people would miss, he needed to fine tune his listening in the same way he needed to continue fine tuning the lithographometer. The caves found in this part of the Ozarks were more famous than the ones he had been to, including Merrimac Caverns. No earthquake had closed it and after speaking with the director, he was provided an escort to take him into a section still under development. The lights and railings had been installed, but it had not been approved for entrance to the general public. This time the machine worked without a flaw and Broadspeare picked up nothing unusual.

When he drove into Ste. Genevieve, the snow had turned to rain and he wished that he had told Claude to change the windshield wipers. He followed the signs pointing to the ferry crossing. The cold rain drenched him when he got out and bought his ticket. The ticket seller told him to hurry since the weather wasn't getting any better and the captain wanted to take off.

When he pulled onto the ferry ramp, a wiry man with a toothless grin dressed in a soiled yellow slicker waved him on. "Git yer ass on board. I shouldn't be making this run except Blevins hates it when we don't git our fill of runs in. Just because he was in the NFL, he thinks he can control the weather and the river. Shit, this river don't pay attention to nobody, and he'll just as likely git us killed than anything. Wish the hell my brother hadn't sold his share of the boat out."

Blevins and the NFL. Broadspeare hoped it wasn't the same man. He pulled on a raincoat and got out of the car. The ferry pitched under his feet. He clung to the railing and made his way to the man in the slicker. "Are you the captain?"

"Damn right. And if'n I owned the whole damned boat, we wouldn't have made this run and you and me would be cozy warm back there."

"You were talking about Blevins. You don't mean a great big man, do you?"

"Big ain't the half of it. And as black as the river is now." He pointed out to the river. Troy's eyes followed his finger and then looked farther up the river. "What's that?" he said pointing to dark mass on the water.

"Grain barge. Surprised to see it out here now. You'd think they would have put in by now. They don't like it when the river is this high."

Troy watched the barge that sat low in the water, like a low mountain by the ocean's edge, absorbing the waves without notice. The longer he watched the, the closer the barge came, getting larger and larger. The captain swore at the barge, at Blevins, and at the river before he shouted a warning that the barge broke loose. He spun the wheel and bellowed, "Hang on tight, we're almost to shore." He spun the wheel back, gunned the engines and aimed the ferry towards the dock on the Illinois side. Troy grabbed for the rail, but his hand slipped off the wet iron. The shoreline was getting closer and closer when the wave hit from behind and Troy was pitched forward, over the side, just as the ferry hit the dock. The captain threw him a life ring. The chill of the river knocked the breath out of him as he reached for the ring, not knowing if he had grabbed it or not. His clothing pulled him down under the water, and his feet slipped on the muddy bottom.

"There he is," someone shouted. "Grab him." Troy, pulled from the river first by his collar, then his waist, was drug out of the river.

"That river's damn cold this time of year. Get him somewhere warm."

"How about Gretchen's place? Throw him in the back of the truck. I don't want him to get everything all wet. The dog'll keep him company. It's only a few hundred yards down the road."

Troy was plopped into the back of the pick up among a pile of tarps. A large dog sniffed him and licked his face as the truck rumbled down the road. The rain felt like pellets of ice stinging his face while he shivered uncontrollably.

"Here you go, mister. That ain't too bad with Skippy taking good care of you. Come on, we'll get you inside and warmed up. I pulled your keys from your pockets and sent the boy to get your car. Don't worry none. Gretchen's boy's a good driver." Troy leaned into the accent and it swirled around his ears—German, no; Southern Illinois, no; Latin. "I've got to be hallucinating."

"Gretchen, this passenger of Beauregard's fell into the river. We got to get him warmed up damn quick. You still got any of Hank's old clothes? Yah? Go get 'em. We'll get him outta these wet things. Into the bathroom with you."

Gretchen's Place was a small tavern and it went by in a blur as Troy was pulled into the men's room. He started to pull of his clothes but shivered too hard.

"Yah, I'll help you. Out of the river, out of the clothes. Here's Gretchen with some dry ones. Hank was her husband. He died last month, but not in these clothes." The man laughed at his own joke.

With the wet clothes off and the dry on, he finally stopped shivering and could focus on his rescuer. The first thought that crossed his mind was Elmer Fudd in his flannel cap with the ear flaps pulled down along with a matching flannel shirt.

"Give me your clothes and I'll run them over to the laundromat. I bet Gretchen's got a coffee for you with a little boost to boot. Come on."

Troy stepped out of the restroom and into the eyes of everyone in the bar. Their eyes scanned him from top to bottom and a few chuckled until a sharp cough from the woman behind the bar cut them off. She must be Gretchen. Troy looked down and saw his ankles and wrists sticking out from the cuffs of the pants and sleeves. He would have laughed as well. He sat down in a chair that was pulled out for him. The woman at the table leaned over and apologized, "We're sorry mister. We didn't mean to laugh, but you look so damned silly in those clothes."

Gretchen brought over a cup of coffee. When Troy brought it to his nose, he smelled the strong, bracing brandy. Both coffee and brandy warmed him. The woman sitting beside him sniffed the air and smelled the brandy as well.

"Hey, Gretchen," she called across the barroom, "when did you get a license for real booze and not just beer and wine."

"It's only for medicinal purposes, and I didn't sell it to him. And no, you don't get any either. I'm not risking my license for the likes of you. You want another wine highball?"

Before Troy's table partner could answer, the door opened, and the ferry boat captain rushed in with Gretchen's son, scanned the room, and hurried over to Troy.

"We got yer car off nice and safe. She's parked outside. I filled her with gas and checked the tires and oil for you. No charge. You going to be okay, mister? I don't want no trouble. I'm really sorry about your going into the river and everything. Most folks just sit in their cars when we cross the river, especially when it's shit weather like tonight. If you'd have stayed in your car, not of this would have happened." He pulled a pint bottle from his pocket. Before he could unscrew the cap, Gretchen yelled out, "Put that away. I ain't gonna lose my license over you, Beauregard. If you need a beer, I'll sell it to you."

"Sorry, Gretchen, I don't mean no trouble. It's just that if Blevins hears word about this, my ass is in the wringer, or worse."

"I'll buy your beer," offered Troy.

"That's mighty nice, mister."

Gretchen caught Troy's nod and poured a glass from the single tap rising from the middle of the bar and set it on the bar. The ferry captain grabbed it, took a long swallow, and said, "Thank you, mister. You're not going to file a complaint with Blevins, are you? From what you said in the ferry, you seem to know him."

"Let's just say I ran into him once."

The man in the Elmer Fudd cap returned and joined Troy. "Your clothes will be dry damn quick. The laundromat's got fast driers. At least the town still has that."

"Not for long," said Gretchen, leaning forward on the bar. "I hear that Blevins made the Widow Kovaks an offer on the place."

"If he did, that will be the end of it. She needs the money," said the woman at Troy's table.

"I don't know why you keep bad-mouthing Blevins," said a younger man who had been listening in from his perch at the bar. He stood out from the rest, dressed in khaki pants and a button-down shirt instead of the jeans and flannels worn by the rest of the patrons. "I think he's bringing some new opportunities into the area. Look what he's been doing down by New Madrid."

"Don't pay attention to that," said Fudd. "I know what he's done up by my place in Cahokia and it's never turned out any good. He's so crooked that when they bury him, they'll have to dig his grave with a corkscrew." He made the gesture of screwing his body into the ground.

"Cahokia?" said Troy. "I'm headed for Cahokia."

"You wouldn't happen to be a Dr. Broadspeare, would you?"

"Yes, why?"

Fudd rose from the table and stuck out his hand, "I'm Amsdorfer. Felix Amsdorfer."

Troy shook his hand, a large, rough hand, strong and knobby like an oak, a farmer's hand. Troy returned the man's grip with as much strength as he could bear. "Welsey sent me down to meet the ferry when she found out that she couldn't make it—some kind of family business, I guess."

"You know Welsey"

"Oh, heavens, yes. Since she was a little girl. She used to wander my farm picking up arrow heads after I disked."

Grumblings rose from the guys at the bar.

"And that don't mean I'm a stranger around here, neither. My family's had a fishing shack on the river ever since we came here from the old country. And that would have been around '48."

"Right after the war?" Troy asked.

"No, 1848. They came with the rest of the bunch that was kicked out of Germany. Nobody liked their politics. Too radical, I guess."

"And some ideas live on in the blood, you old Democrat," said one of the men sitting at the bar.

"Don't pay any attention to him, Dr. Broadspeare. I've been sparring with that old Republican for so long that we're just used to it."

The bar door opened, and a blast of cold air sent fresh shivers through Broadspeare. An old woman wearing only a shawl came in carrying a pile of neatly folded clothes.

"He's over there," said Gretchen pointing at Broadspeare. "The one in my Hank's old clothes with his arms and legs sticking out."

"The wind done took the warmth out of them, I'm afraid. They so nice and toasty when I took them out of the dryer a minute ago. How this cold gets into my old bones. At least this is my last winter here. Thanks to Mr. Blevins, I'm moving to Florida as soon as I can find a place down there."

"You must be Mrs. Kovaks," said Broadspeare, rising to accept his clothes. "Thank you for bringing my clothes over. I could have come for them myself."

She handed him the clothes and looked him over from head to foot. "Not dressed like that. No siree. Not like that." She laughed, and everyone joined in.

He took them and went into the restroom, changed, and came out with Hank's clothes, thanking Gretchen for their use.

"We can spend the night in my fishing shack. It's about a mile up the river, but five by the road."

The rain had turned to ice and a thin layer covered Felix' truck as well as Troy's car.

"Follow me to the shack but be careful on that ice."

The Amsdorfer shack lived up to the name, being a patch on patch collection of walls, windows, and roof lines. The stumps of concrete foundations showed where parts of the building had been torn down. Piles of lumber sticking out from under tarpaulins revealed some project of renewal.

The interior contrasted sharply with the exterior for it was neat, tidy, and contained the last thing Troy expected: a well-stocked bookcase. Curiosity drew him to scan the titles and he found a reflection of his father's books, like Virgil's Aeneid, and others.

"When the fish don't bite, it's a good time to read," said Felix.

"I know some of these." Troy pulled the Aeneid off the shelf, opened it, and exclaimed, "This is in Latin."

"Well, yeah. We're not all dumb farmers over here. My father taught me the way his father taught him, and his before him. Don't you know the history of the Latin farmers of Illinois?" Felix explained that when the 48ers, as they were known, emigrated to America many were radical professors who took up farming but didn't want to give up their studies. The struggled in the new world to keep their old ways with the final remnant passing on their libraries and languages.

"And did you teach your children?" Troy said.

"No. I'm sad to say that Martha and I didn't have any. But I'm proud to say that I passed it on to Welsey. She took to it *celerius quam asparagi cocuntur*. You best get some rest; you've got a busy day tomorrow. I wasn't planning on spending the night down here, so we'll have to leave a bit early."

The Great River Road followed the Illinois side of the Mississippi over the floodplains of rich farmland and passing through small towns whose names reflected the European settlers who created their colonies, towns with French names like Du Pere, German like Wittenberg, or English like Quincy. Troy followed Amsdorfer's truck through these towns until they arrived at a place named for the Indian tribe—Cahokia.

Amsdorfer drove into Cahokia Mounds State Park, parked his truck in the visitor's lot, got out, and motioned to Troy to park next to his truck. Other than a few vehicles in the employee's lot, theirs were the only vehicles in the park. Troy looked across the lot and his eyes followed a shapely woman in a tailored park ranger uniform to the front door of a large building labeled

"Museum and Welcome Center." She unlocked the door and went in.

"Now we can go on in. How much do you know about Cahokia Mounds?" asked Amsdorfer. Troy shook his head.

"I didn't think so. She'll fill you in. She's expecting you. Her name's Evelyn Tolkens and she runs the place. I got to get back to the farm. If you look past that round mound." he pointed off into the distance. Troy followed the line of his finger, past a hump in the middle of the grassy meadow of the park and into a field that lay bare except for the melting layer of sleet on the downed cornstalks. "That's my farm. Welsey should be by a little before noon." He climbed into his truck and drove off, his dog sitting by his side.

The wind blew cold under Broadspeare's coat and he pulled it tighter around himself while he crossed the parking lot. He was too cold to notice the much other than the tall mount at the end of a long walkway that extended beyond the museum. Ranger Tolkens was waiting for him. She looked like she worked out in the gym several hours each day and her uniform was far from standard state issue. She wore her blonde hair pulled back for business and her blue eyes shone from behind her glasses.

"You must be Dr. Broadspeare. I understand that you'll be conducting research here. If I can be of any assistance, let me know."

Troy considered asking her to button one more button on her blouse but changed his mind.

"We're very proud of our museum, especially with the recent addition." She pointed to the new construction that still carried the scent of fresh paint.

He noticed the large sign designating the donor: Demetrius Blevins.

"Cahokia Mounds State Park," she said, slipping into tour guide mode, "was the center of one of the largest cities of its time, larger than its contemporary, London. The Cahokia Empire of indigenous woodland dwellers stretched up and down the fertile flood plain of the Mississippi. They were an agrarian culture, finding the plains an easy place to grow their main crops: corn and beans. The mounds we see today are a small portion of those built when the city was in its prime. The most notable one remaining is Monks Mound." Through the large window he saw it rising from the plain.

"Monks Mound," she continued, "is the largest earthen structure of its kind in the world. The city was led by kings and their priests who built temples and dwelling on top of the mounds, some of which, unfortunately, have been torn away by European settlers. None of the mounds remain on the Missouri side of the river since the builders of St. Louis found them to be a ready source of fill dirt. Many around here were leveled to make way for the subdivisions as the local towns grew."

She turned from her spot by the window and walked into the museum. Troy followed. "We believe that the inhabitants of Mound City lived in an egalitarian culture with the king as first among equals. Our dioramas portray their life together."

"Ms. Tolkens, what is known about their language?"

"Nothing, absolutely nothing. They left no written records and the tribes the Europeans met came after the city had fallen to ruins."

'What about the Cahokia Tribe?"

"They arrived much later, and their language was Algonquin."

"For all we know," Troy offered, "the original inhabitants, the kings and priests, could have spoken Mayan, or Aztec, or Latin."

"We doubt if it was any of those, especially Latin, Dr. Broadspeare, since those all have written forms. Like I said, their language is a complete mystery, but that's why you're here, isn't it. May I call you Troy?" She reached out and gently squeezed his arm.

"Dr. Broadspeare!" cried someone from behind him. He turned around and saw the girl whose picture he had taken from Facebook several months before. "Dr. Broadspeare! There you are." Welsey Yergens strode through the maze of exhibits straight for him.

Evelyn Tolkens stared at her and then Troy, arching an eyebrow. "Do you know her?"

"Yes, but we haven't officially met."

Welsey marched past Tolkens to Troy and shook his hand. "Am I glad to catch you here. I'm sorry I couldn't meet you in Modoc, but considering what happened there, it turned out to be a good thing that I wasn't there. I wouldn't have known what do like Felix did."

"If I could continue" Tolkens barked, pointing to the wall-sized map in the museum. "We found in that village over there a large number of flint chippings, a larger number than most, so we believe that this village would have been like a factory for the manufacture of arrowheads. This other one bore strong signs of fiber work for the making of cloth. In other words, a very advanced system of specialization."

"They must have had an advanced bureaucracy to coordinate all that," said Troy.

"Or a dictatorship," added Welsey.

Tolkens turned to her and barked, "Young lady, I know all about that theory and the evidence doesn't support it."

Suddenly, the shaking of the building and the rattling of the windows stopped their conversation.

"Earthquakes aren't common here, are they?" he asked.

"No," said Tolkens, pulling herself into official status. "This region has been quiet for more than a hundred years. This is most unusual, I assure you, Dr. Broadspeare."

"But what about the New Madrid quake?" said Welsey.

The front door opened, and a bus load of tourists entered and began milling around. "If you will excuse me," said Tolkens. She strode off to the front door, buttoning her blouse as she went.

"Yes, what about the New Madrid quake?" he asked.

Welsey leaned towards him and whispered, "We need to get out of here. I'll tell you at my place."

He followed her through the exhibits and out into the parking lot. Her ancient Geo Tracker made his Ford wagon look new. She opened the door, pulled out a blanket and wrapped it around her legs like a skirt. "The heater doesn't work very well, and the little bit of heat that does come out can't match the drafts through the floorboard. But she starts every time and goes just about anywhere."

The "anywhere" Welsey led Troy was the inner city of East St. Louis. Long the second cousin to the larger city across the river, East St. Louis earned its reputation as a city in trouble and wracked with poverty. From the race riots of the '60s to the abandonment by the industries, the meat packing houses, and the stockyards, the city looked like it had long given up on hope, and the building she pulled her Tracker next to appeared to have borne the brunt of the decay on its own. She pulled in between the rusting hulk of a Cadillac and a pick-up truck on cinder blocks. He wondered why in the world she would be taking him to this place.

"I'll bet this isn't what you were expecting," she said while unlocking the padlock on the door.

"You could say that." Packets of trash, windblown litter, and the rare clump of weeds breaking the remnants of sidewalk surrounded him.

"It's a lot safer than it looks, and the rent is next to nothing."

"I should hope so. Are we going to be here long? If we are, I want to get a few things from the car."

"Considering the neighborhood, that would be a good idea." She put her shoulder to the door and pushed, the bottom of the door dragging across the concrete threshold. Troy grabbed his lithographometer and suitcase and followed her in. The ragged door masked an interior with a second door, one more substantial as if the outer shell of the building was simply that, a shell around a better building. Light came down from a skylight that bore the marks of recent repair with the fresh paint around the trim a marked contrast to the flaps of peeling paint hanging beside it.. Welsey opened the door to what once had been an office lobby decorated into a living space.

"Not much, I know, but it fits my needs." She pointed to a room labeled "Accounting" and in it he found a cot, desk, chair, and pegs to hang clothes. "If you'd rather stay in a hotel, I wouldn't be offended. This place makes strange noises at night, but you get used to it after a while.

"Do you really live here?"

"And work here. I'll show you why back here." She opened a door to a long hallway line with doors. Pairs of broken light fixtures grew from the wall, one red and the other green, hanging over each door.

"This used to be a radio station, and then a recording studio. For a while they held music lessons in the broadcast booths. Most of them are shot except for this one." She opened the door revealing a room fitted out with state of the art recording and play-back equipment. Racks held hundreds of white boxes containing old tape recordings. Next to them were even older celluloid disks in tattered cardboard sleeves. This is where she had been doing her research, where she had made the recording that enticed him to leave Kansas. He sighed in approval. "Where did you get all this?" He ran his hand over the equipment, then bent over to study of the machines. "This must have cost a fortune. The university doesn't even have one of these."

"If you think this is something, look at this." She unlocked a door as heavy as one on a safe.

"Don't tell me, the archives." He walked into a large room lined from floor to ceiling with shelves filled with recordings. "There must be thousands in here. How far back do they go?"

Some date back to the first radio broadcasts in the Mississippi Valley. News broadcasts, commercials, everything. This is how I found the changes."

"How?"

"I followed your theories, Dr. Broadspeare."

"You really have been, haven't you?"

"You sound surprised."

He was. While litholinguistics was his life's work, he never thought anyone would follow up on him. Yet her she was, this young woman. How old was she? Maybe 28? He noticed the same excitement he must have shown to Nashure Keene when they first met and Troy went traipsing after him into Tuscany to trace language roots in Etruscan tombs.

She showed him the geological map of the area taped over the window that the radio engineers would once have used, and how she had laid out the major formations of the substrata. Running through the map was a jagged line like a lightning bolt splitting it two. She said that it was the New Madrid Fault.

"I keep hearing about this New Madrid Fault since I left Kansas, but what is it?" He took out his pen and used it as a pointer to follow the jagged line on the map.

"That's quite a pen," she said.

"It's special. I use it for grading. Now what about the fault?"

"It's the same as the San Andreas only it hasn't shifted in more than a hundred years. If it ever does, watch out. The last time it shifted, the earthquake was so intense that portions of the Mississippi River flowed backwards. It was felt all the way to the East Coast. The only reason the damage wasn't greater is because not many people lived here then. If an earthquake like that would hit now, it would be worse than the one in San Francisco in 1906."

"Could it be shifting now? I've been feeling a lot of quakes lately. One nearly trapped me in a cavern about a week ago. But what does this have to do with Cahokia?"

"I can tell you don't know much about this area, do you?" He nodded in agreement, saying that he had been raised and educated in Europe.

"Most Americans, even those in the Midwest don't know about it. That's why the state put up the museum. Unfortunately, it's full of lies."

"How?"

"What Ranger Tolkens told you is nonsense. The people who lived here didn't live in peaceful coexistence. That's for the tourists. The kings and priests dominated the region. They were like the Aztecs with their human sacrifice. When the archeologists excavated Mound 76 they found the skeletons of dozens of people, many of them with their skulls bashed in laying in a tumbled heap in the bottom of the grave. Do you think they want to put that out for the tourists or the school kids on a class trip? During high school I worked at the park and was told never to mention the sacrifices, and if someone should ask about them, to explain they were rare. That isn't true."

"Is that how you know so much about it?"

"I was raised here, Dr. Broadspeare. This is my home. Mr. Amsdorfer let me wander through his fields looking for arrowheads. A lot has been explained about this place, except for one unsolved mystery."

"Which is what?"

"What happened to it? Why did it end so suddenly? Why was there no residual memory of it; no tales about it in the stories of the Native Americans who came after? It's like the mound builders never were here and these mounds just grew from the soil. That mystery took me to your research hoping I could find traces of their language in the way people around here speak."

For the next three weeks, Troy Broadspeare and Welsey Yergens listened to old recordings of radio broadcasts, paying special attention to the guests being interviewed and the locals who made their own commercials since the professional broadcasters all sounded like they came from nowhere. They nailed down the shifts of tone and rhythm, but it wasn't enough.

This isn't working," Troy said, jerking off the headphones.

"Be careful with those," she barked. "They have to be working. Give them to me."

"The headphones are fine. That's not what's wrong. Something's not quite there. I think I'm getting closer, that I'm getting the hint of another, older language buried in the sounds, but it's like glimpsing the sharp reflection of the needle in the haystack only to see it disappear again."

"We need a break, Dr. Broadspeare. We've been inside for too long."

They left the lab to prowl the area around the park. Troy lugged his equipment along, "just in case." Since Felix Amsdorfer's farm lay next to the park, they focused there, thankful for the late January thaw.

"They tell me that once a mound was here," said Amsdorfer, pointing to a slight rise in the meadow. "Let me show you. Come on, Skippy," he called to the dog and the four of them crossed the field. When they approached the mound, the dog ran ahead and began growling and digging. "What's up old boy, find another ground hog?" Before Amsdorfer could reach the dog, he stumbled over the sharp edge of a stone breaking through the soil. "I may be getting old, but I could have sworn that stone wasn't there last summer. It must have heaved during the winter." He gave the stone a deliberate kick and quickly jumped back, holding his foot. "I think I broke it. Not the stone, my foot."

Troy tried to nudge the stone with his foot. Nothing happened. He got on his hands and knees to examine it, then motioned Welsey to join him. "It's new stone—a fresh break with little sign of erosion, which is odd," she said.

She dug her hands into the cold, wet dirt around the stone and pulled to expose more of it. Troy opened his case and took out one of the forks, thumped it on his hand, and set it on the stone. Nothing. He worked his way down the line of forks until he found the one that resonated with the crystalline structure of the minerals within the stone.

"That's strange, very strange, indeed. This doesn't match any known language in North America."

"Which means what?"

"Either this stone came from somewhere else, or the people who spoke the language of this stone did. We need to expose more of the stone. Felix, do you have a shovel?"

"Yah, in the barn. I'll get it. It may take a while since I crippled up my foot on that thing. Be good to get it out of here anyway before spring."

Troy and Welsey continued clawing away at the dirt, examining the stone as they went, ignoring the damp ground soaking their clothes. Troy felt, for the first time, an ache that his father complained of. The rumble of a tractor echoed from the barn. They looked and saw Felix driving a front-end loader filled with shovels and rakes.

"If we need to move a lot of dirt," he said by way of explanation.

They each took a shovel and began digging a trench around the stone, quickly discovering that the stone was like an iceberg with the tip that Felix tripped over barely hinted at the size that lay below the surface. Felix waved the other two out of the way, climbed onto the loader, lowered the blade, and pulled off a load of dirt. Frost lay bare in the hole, frost that the sun quickly melted and pooled at the bottom of the hole. He worked his way around the stone, excavating a broad, encircling ditch, three feet deep with no end in sight. Troy signaled for him to stop and turn off the engine. He took out his forks and again tested the stone. "That's even stranger," he said, working down the line of forks.

"What's stranger?"

"Oh, sorry. I was talking to myself. Now, I'm getting a different set of resonances. Some are more local. It's almost as if this stone contains several disconnected languages. That's impossible, but here it is."

"Hey, Dr. Broadspeare," said Felix from the other side of the stone. "If you think that's strange, look at this. There's something at the bottom. Let me try and get it."

Troy and Welsey watched from their side of the stone. They could see his head and shoulders while he worked the shovel, dirt flying over his shoulder onto the meadow. "It looks like some kind of ..." A tremor rattled through the meadow. Felix screamed and disappeared from sight. Skippy started to bark while Troy and Welsey clambered over from their side, slipping in the cold, wet mud. She shivered as the damp soaked her clothes.

"Felix," she said, "are you all right?"

They found him sitting in the bottom of the hole with his right leg under the stone. The dog busily licking his face.

"Skippy, that's enough. I'm fine. Yah, I think I'm okay, but this rock's got something in for my leg. Get me out of here."

They slipped down into the hole and struggled to pull him up by the armpits. Before they could pull him free, the earth shook, and the stone twisted, grinding against his leg. He let out a scream that shattered against the stone. The stone stopped. She looked at him and said, "Felix, did you do that?"

"Do what?"

"The stone was moving until you screamed and then it stopped," she said.

Troy clawed his way out of the holed and returned with the set of tuning forks. "Felix, could you scream again?" he said, holding one of the forks against the stone and pointing it at Felix.

"I don't know where that first one came from, but I'll give 'er a try." He screamed, and Troy shook his head. They tried it again with a second fork with no success. They went through the collection of forks with Troy urging Felix to keep screaming until the old man complained that his throat was getting sore. "And I hate to be a party pooper, but my leg's gone numb."

They tried and again to pull him from the hole, he told Welsey to get the loader.

Troy cast a quizzical look at him.

"How do you think she paid for her Latin lessons? She's a good hard worker around the farm."

She edged the loader towards Felix and Troy, lowering the bucket.

"Bring it down a little closer," Felix said. "Dr. Broadspeare, you get in the bucket and hold on to me." Troy wedged himself into the bucket and Felix laid across him the best he could. "You got a good grip on me?" Troy nodded. "All right, take her up, nice and easy."

Welsey gunned the engine and nudged bucket up. Felix grimaced, and she stopped.

"What'd you stop for?" he called out. "Try again.

The engine growled and the bucket slowly rose taking Troy and Felix with it. A loud sucking sound came from the hole with Felix and his leg. She backed the loader free from the hole and lowered the bucket. Troy helped Felix to his feet and steadied him while he tested the leg.

"Nothing's broken. But I lost a good shoe." Troy looked down and Felix waved his stocking foot, the red toe of the monkey sock showing through the layer of caked mud. Troy left him with the loader and went down into the hole to find the shoe. The ground where Felix had been trapped had caved in, revealing a larger hole. Troy took one of the shovels and poked it down the hole as far as he could. No bottom. Then he took a clod of dirt and tossed it in, expecting to hear a splat or a splash. No sound came back. Welsey came to his side and peered into the hole. Skippy came near her and barked at the opening.

"What is it? Some kind of sinkhole?"

"If it was a sinkhole, how could that great big stone just sit there?"

Grey clouds moved in, covering the sun. The temperature dropped, and a cold drizzle fell. The chill that had been hunting them worked its way into their bones. Felix climbed onto the loader and told them to throw the shovels into the loader and climb on board. Troy cradled the case of tuning forks under one arm and held on with the other as the loader rolled through the meadow into the barn with the dog running along side.

The drizzle turned into rain mixed with snow by the time they made it into Felix's house. All four were soaked.

"This is the second time I've had to dry you off, Dr. Broadspeare. I hope this isn't going to be a common occurrence."

Felix set out a bottle of brandy on the kitchen table before going off to find dry clothes for them. After they had changed into the dry clothes Felix said that since it would take a while to wash and dry them, they might as well help themselves to the brandy. "I'd tell you to make yourselves at home, but that wouldn't mean much to Welsey since she already does that most of the time."

Troy poured about two fingers worth into the glasses and handed one to her. "You two seem to have quite a relationship."

"He has been like a father to me; no, more than a father, ever since I wandered into his fields when I was a little girl. We used to live over there." She pointed to the west. "Where that strip-mall is now going up, my house used to be. I must have looked like such a little ragamuffin with my hair in pigtails and dressed in little girl overalls. It's a wonder he didn't run me off." She took a sip and looked down the hall for Felix's return. "I guess he was lonely. He used to be a high school Latin teacher. He used to tell me that I was his very last student." She took another sip and laughed. "I don't know which was harder, learning to drive the tractor or conjugating verbs."

"And sometimes, young lady, I made you do both at the same time. Where's the brandy? I guess you didn't hear me come up." Troy poured him a glass, handed it to him, and he took a large gulp. "That'll warm me up fast." He sat down with them, propped his elbows on the table and said, "Yah, she was my last student. One of the best, too. I just wish I could have convinced her to finish that master's degree, so she could get on with her doctorate."

"Please, don't go there again."

"I'm sorry. I promised you that I wouldn't and I'll live up to my promise." He looked into the glass before taking a sip from the little remaining. "Maybe we'd better change the subject." He shifted his chair to face Troy. "What I want to know is what happened out there. And what was it with all those tuning forks and my screaming my lungs out. I hope they neighbors didn't hear. They already think I'm crazy."

Troy told him about his research into the subterranean vibrations' influence the language of the people living in a given area and that different rock formations, because of varying mineral content, give out different vibrations theoretically making it possible to trace the languages that were spoken in earlier times through the linguistic variations of any given place.

"You mean to say, Dr. Broadspeare, that it's the rocks that give us our language"

"In part, but only in part. Not the meanings of the words, but the vibrations that create the sounds we build into language. It's not the words and sentences, but the how of the words and sentences."

"Then what about my screaming at the tuning forks?"

Troy reached for his case and showed it to Amsdorfer. "This was made for my old professor, Dr. Nashau Keene. He spent his entire life listening to the vibrations and tuning these forks to what he heard." He opened the case, lifted one out and held it for Felix to take. "Do you know music, Mr. Amsdorfer?"

"Yah, I used to play the fiddle good enough for square dances. But one thing before we go on. If you're going to be wearing my clothes, call me Felix."

"Then listen to the fork and tell me what you hear."

Felix thumped it against his palm and held it to his ear. "This thing is off-key."

"For music, yes, but not for languages. Welsey, when I ask you to, tell me a nursery rhyme, anyone. But first drain you glass so you can speak into it." She drained her glass and he did the same. They set their glasses on the table, close but not touching. He pointed to her, tapped the fork, and held it to his glass.

She recited, "Jack be nimble, Jack be quick, Jack jump over. . . "She stopped and stared at the glasses as did Felix. Both glasses rattled on the table with a distinctive tone rising from each of them, lasting a long as the fork vibrated.

"This fork is tuned to the common substrata of this area. When you spoke into the glass, you created the vibrations of the substrata. I matched it with my glass and set up a sympathetic vibration. Since mine was stronger and more concentrated, it took over."

"But what about my screaming?" asked Felix.

"That's the problem. It didn't match any of my forks and yet, it seemed to have stopped the shifting of that stone."

"Are you saying that the stone isn't from here?" asked Welsey.

"That doesn't seem possible," said Felix. "Look at the size of that thing. It would have crushed my leg if it had shifted any more. Something that big doesn't just get up and move around on its own. It had to be moved."

"Yes, it had to be moved, but when, why, and how?" asked Troy.

"Sleep often gives answers when daylight hides them," said Felix. "I've plenty of rooms in this old house and you're more than welcome to stay. That weather doesn't sound none too good anyway."

Troy looked out the window and watched the sleet build a layer of ice on his car. He looked at Welsey. She was wrapped in an old robe, one that Felix said had belonged to his mother. An old-fashioned robe, warm, comfortable, and sensible except for the lace trim around the neck and wrists. Why drag her out into the cold? She looked at him and her brown eyes deepened in the desire to stay, and he saw no need to break it.

"If it's all right with Welsey, we'll stay."

"And besides," she added, "When the weather breaks, we can get back to the stone that much earlier."

Chapter 5

The rain stopped in the night and when the sun rose, it sparkled through the ice that covered the branches of the trees, turning them into crystal that would melt into the day.

The sleet had also turned the meadow into an ice pond that they slipped and slid across in their approach to the stone that seemed to have risen a bit higher, even the dog had a difficult time of it. When they arrived at the stone, they saw that the hole Felix had fallen into had widened and deepened from the rain washing down.

"What happened to all the dirt?" Welsey asked.

"It's down there." Troy shined his flashlight into the hole. The light followed a slope leading under the stone and disappeared into the darkness.

"That's not the only thing. Look what else the rain washed up," said Felix waving his shovel at the base of the stone. Where a thick layer of mud had been, the bright stone reflected the morning light and on what looked like carved markings.

"I'm going to take a look," said Troy. He stepped off the grassy edge of the meadow and onto the muddy slope of the whole.

"Be careful, Troy," said Welsey.

He looked up at her and said, "What happened to calling me Dr. Broadspeare?"

"Please. Just be careful. At least take my hand."

He took her hand and leaned towards the markings. "They're not natural, I can tell by the regularity of the carving. but I can't decipher them.

They make no sense at all." He took out his pocket knife and scrapped away the dirt.

"Then trade places with me," said Welsey. "You forget that this is my specialty."

They switched places and she peered at the markings. "No wonder you didn't recognize them. These are North American glyphs, and not very common at that, although some of the motifs and techniques are the same as the Aztec."

"Are you starting to lecture me, Ms. Yergens?

"No, Doctor. Well, yes, but it's because I know more about this place than you do. If you look at the lines here . . ." She pointed towards a particular glyph.

"I can't tell what you are pointing at."

"Then give me a little slack, edge a bit closer."

He shifted to get closer and suddenly the unstable mud gave way under his feet. He fell on his backside and slid down into the hole, taking Wesley with him.

"What the hell do you think you're doing?" came Wesley's cry from deep within the hole.

"Could you move?" said Troy. Enough light shone through the opening to light the space they had fallen into.

"Are you two all right?" called Felix down the hole. "Skippy, get back from there.

"We'd be better if Dr. Broadspeare wasn't on top of me."

"Anything broken?" Felix urgently called.

"We landed onto the mud and it broke our fall."

"Don't tell me you're soaking wet again, Dr. Broadspeare?" said Felix.

"Him and me both," said Welsey.

"It looks like I better get some rope."

Welsey took the light from Troy and shined it up to the stone. "There's more of them. They run along here." She used the light to follow the line of glyphs down the side of the stone and into the mud on the floor of the cave.

"I wonder where they go?" asked Troy, speaking as much to himself as to Wesley. "Shine the light over there."

She shone the light in the direction he pointed to, and it hit a wall. The light reflected off the water seeping through the rock face and running down like tears.

"We could call it the Weeping Wall," she said.

"Maybe somebody already has. Look in the upper corner. I think I saw something."

She moved the light to the corner and there, covered with a thin layer of limestone, was a hand, a human hand looking like it was reaching out from the wall.

"We're not the first to be down here."

Troy took the light from her and moved closer to the hand. It looked like it was growing from the wall— where the wrist met the wall, a line like a fissure ran directly across to the stone.

"It looks like it was trapped in the rock and tried to get out," she said. "And look above the hand, where the stone is dry. I can almost make the glyphs out. 'the hand that guards the waters…' I can't make more out without better light."

"One more impossible event to add to the lengthy list. What's over there?" Troy stepped out of the circle of light under the hole's opening and into the darkness.

"You're not going to leave me, are you?"

"Come on, then." He put out his hand for her and she clasped it. "It's like ice," he said. Through her fingers he felt her shivering. "You're cold."

"Yes," she said through chattering teeth.

He pulled her into his arms and held her, rubbing her back and arms to warm her. When she put her arms tightly around him, he forgot about the cave and instead, how to get out of there.

"I'm all right," she said, pulling away from him, still shivering. "Thanks. Now, what else is here?"

They hadn't gone very far when they heard Felix call down from above. "You two still down there? I got the rope and the tractor, too." A thick rope fell, hanging into the cave. Soon they were out of the cave and above ground. A cold wind blew from the north. Welsey shook uncontrollably. "We've got to get her out of here and back to the house," said Troy.

Sitting on the seat of the tractor, Felix said, "Put her on my lap. Come on, Welsey, it will be just like old times. Hang on tight." He gunned the engine and drove as fast as he could over the frozen meadow, bouncing from rut to rut.

Troy was left in the confusion of his thoughts while he trudged to Amsdorfer's house, rubbing his arms to keep the circulation going and trying to keep his mind off the chill working its way through his muddy and wet clothes. When he focused on what he had glimpsed in the cave, the glyphs, the fossilized hand, and what lay in the deeper darkness, his mind kept going to Welsey, hoping that she would be all right.

By the time he reached the house, he could barely lift one foot high enough to clear the ground, and more than once, stumbled. When he reached the door, he caught Felix coming out.

"I was on my way to get you," he said. We got to get you out of those clothes. I'm running out of clothes for you, though. I don't run a haberdashery, you know. All that's left is a robe of my sister and a blanket." He wagged a finger at Troy. "This is the last time. Three times is enough, Doctor." He sighed and added, "Unless I have to do it again. You know where the washer is by now. Just put your clothes in there.

Amsdorfer's sister must have been a large woman because her robe fit Troy except for the length. He wrapped the blanket around his waist to make up for the deficit and went into the kitchen where Felix was heating soup.

"She's going to be fine. Stuck her in a warm bath right away." He turned from the stove and glared at Troy. "And don't even think of looking at me like that. She's as much as a daughter to me as her own parents, maybe better. She's all tucked into a warm bed and needs this soup. I suppose there's enough for us, too." He poured two mugs and handed the second to Troy. "Canned tomato. You can't expect much from an old bachelor. I'll be right back." He picked up the first and carried out of the kitchen. Then it dawned on Troy what little he knew about Wesley Yergens. While some would label her African-American, her features refused to match any stereotype. Her accent didn't completely fit, either, even though it was well grounded in the southwestern Illinois variety. Something else was there, a type of refinement, but what? He wasn't often stumped, and this bothered him. One more mystery— one more element that didn't fit in. He took a swallow of soup and its warmth spread through his body. A second gulp and with it, a wave of exhaustion. He shoved the mug to one side and lay his head in the curve of his arm on the table.

"Dr. Broadspeare?"

He pulled the blanket over his head and pushed his face into the pillow to make the question go away.

"Dr. Broadspeare?" Someone pushed against his back and gently rocked him back and forth. He tried to curl up into a ball, but there wasn't enough room and he tumbled onto the floor. He looked up and saw Welsey fully dressed standing over him. He looked around and saw the legs of the couch and the coffee table. "Felix put you on the couch when you fell asleep. You've been sleeping for two hours and we need to get going."

His legs felt cold and he knew his legs were bare. What else crept out from the short robe of Amsdorfer's sister? He sat up with a jolt and pulled the blanket around his legs.

She turned away, so he could get up without embarrassment. When she turned back around she held out his clothes, freshly washed, dried, and folded. He reached out for them, letting the blanket slip. He grabbed it with one hand and the clothes with the other and made his way to the bathroom to dress. As he was dressing he heard sharp words between Welsey and Felix echoing down the hallway.

He came out of the bathroom only to catch Felix glaring at him. Before he could ask what he had done, Felix looked at Welsey and said, "I'm just worried about you, that's all. Your falling into that pit scared me. I don't want you getting into something you can't handle."

She took his hand and gently rubbed it. "Don't worry, Felix, I'll be fine." She rose on her toes and kissed him on the cheek.

"You best go, then," he said, holding the kiss in place with his hand.

The wind still blew from the north driving the January thaw ahead of it. Ice had to be scraped off the car, but at least the road was dry. Troy and Welsey drove back to the former radio station she called home and office. A fresh set of tire tracks lay trapped in the frozen mud.

"Were you expecting visitors?"

"It's probably nothing. Somebody getting lost and turning around."

"Who would be sightseeing down here in a sleet storm?"

She made a comment that he worried too much, "just like Felix," and unlocked the outer door. They pushed it open, stepped inside, and the building shook, rattling the windows.

"Another tremor. You'd think your New Madrid fault was trying to tell us something," he said.

"Maybe it is." She opened the inner door and a scene of chaos greeted them. Books and tapes lay scattered on the floor. Papers littered the desk.

"That tremor we felt yesterday in the meadow must have been stronger here," she said.

"I may be no expert on earthquakes, but I don't think they can open and search drawers. Look at the file cabinet."

The file draws lay half open and the files in disarray.

Staying close together, they searched the rest of the building. Nothing else had been touched.

"Probably looking for something to steal," she said.

"A thief would have taken the electronics, the TV, and the computer. And how did they get in? You had to unlock the doors, remember? And we didn't see any sign of forced entry. They were looking for something. Something having to do with your research. I wonder if anything is missing?"

They spend the rest of the day cleaning up the mess and discovered that little, if anything was missing, and the chaos was less chaotic than believed. "It's more like they wanted to make a mess of things. I don't believe they were looking for anything in particular," she said.

"Why would they—if it is a 'they.' It could a 'he' or a 'she' for all we know. But why make such a mess?" he asked.

"Maybe to scare me off. Or us off. Nobody paid attention to what I was doing until I found out about you, Dr. Troy Broadspeare."

"What does that mean?"

"It means that I could happily spend hours listening to old tapes, monitor the seismograph, look for Native American artifacts and nobody cared. They just dismissed me as some whacko African-American chick who was never black enough or white enough to fit in, who loved science and languages. Then suddenly, people around me changed."

"What do you mean?"

"It's like I was becoming dangerous to them. Threatening." She stopped talking, picked up a folder, riffed through the pages without looking at them, straightened them, and placed them back in the cabinet.

"Who's 'they'?"

"I don't know what you're talking about."

"You talked about becoming dangerous to "them." Who are 'they'?"

"You know, people in general." She looked away from him and said that they shouldn't spend the night there.

Troy agreed and offered to cover her hotel bill, saying he had plenty of grant money, which was partly true, but she declined, reminding him that this was her home town and she could find a place.

"Like family or friends?"

"Something like that." She added that she would call him in the morning; hopefully, with good news.

The hotel was typical of those euphemistically called "budget," with furnishings that have been passed down from the more up-scale chains making into a hand-me-down sort of hotel. The amenities were the same in name only. Instead of the tiny shampoo bottle, he found a packet like ketchup comes in. Six-ounce coffee cups replaced the eight-ounce, and the bedspread carried strong traces of the 80s. At least the room was clean and the water hot. With a sigh of resignation, he hauled his belongings into the room.

The first item on his agenda was the cleaning of the tuning forks. The outing into the muddy meadow left them spotted and stained, causing him to worry about their tuning being affected. He didn't know the exact frequencies that Keene had used to create them, and he knew that once the forks were gone, the secret would be gone with them. He cleared the desk, laid one of the hotel bath towels on it, and with a washcloth methodically polished each one, laying them out in ascending order on the towel. When he turned the case over and tapped it against the towel to know out any remaining dirt, the bottom rattled. Hoping that the travel hadn't damaged it, he inspected the inside. "Damn, I think I broke it." One corner was dislodged. Wondering what it would take to repair it, he slipped the tip of his pocket knife into the crack and carefully pried it up.

It popped clear. Burnt into the wood on the underside were nine musical staves of four lines each. Five of the staves bore notes, the others bare as if waiting for completion.

He then recalled Dr. Keene's late interest in musical composition. At the time, Troy believed this to be an old man's curiosity, some new challenge to keep the mind supple. But here, hidden under the tuning forks, the secreted lines told of something else.

Despite the humbleness of the hotel's amenities, it did provide free wifi and a copier. He used them both, happily paying twenty-five cents each for two copies of the back panel. The wifi connection brought him information about the staves. Even though he told his students to avoid Wikipedia like the plague, he read its article on music and discovered that the four-line staff went out of fashion at about same time as Guttenberg's development of printing. He also realized that Keene's notes, in their shape and arrangement were unlike others he was familiar with, instead of round notes Keene's were squares, rectangles and diamond shaped.

The wifi also delivered an email from Greenefield. She was wondering how he was going on. He wasn't sure how much he should tell her. How much would she believe? He didn't want her to think he had gone insane fanaticizing about a lost Indian empire. He'd never get his old teaching job then. He replied as noncommittally as he could, saying that Welsey was developing into a great research partner and that she had laid a solid foundation from which their work could continue. He was about to add more about the young woman but didn't want to give Avon the impression that he was bragging on her.

January bled into February. Troy and Welsey divided time between the radio station and eavesdropping wherever people gathered. They used their smartphones to record random conversations, developing techniques so they could hold them close to the speaker without getting detected. Using Cahokia Mounds as a center, they drew a series of concentric circles around it and worked inwards. They found coffee shops and bars in outlying town. They crashed funeral luncheons to gather the voices of older generations. Slowly they amassed a database of tones, rhythms, and inflections, searching for any discernable pattern. They ran the recordings through acoustical filters to eliminate all meaning, listening for the deep heartbeat of the language. Troy pointed out what to listen for, what to pay attention to, in the same way Keene had taught him. When she found a pattern of clusters that didn't match their map, he congratulated her.

The final step was to plot their patterns on the geological map and found that yes, they did follow the substrata minerals, but when they attempted the same on the map of ancient Cahokia, a different pattern emerged. Those lying close to the Mounds bore a tonal pattern that contrasted with those of outlying areas. According to Evelyn Tolkens, those outlying areas were feeder villages that provided for the needs of the city.

The gray skies of February continued to hang low over Cahokia when they stopped in to see Felix.

"It's about time. I was wondering whatever happened to you. I was planning on how I was going to fill in that hole so the cattle won't fall in when I turn them out in the meadow."

"Felix, when was the last time you had any cows?" asked Welsey.

"Well, I might get some. With the way the market is these days, I may need to diversify."

Troy remembered how defensive the old man could become concerning Welsey and he wasn't sure how to suggest that they needed to go back into the cave. "You know, Mr. Amsdorfer."

"Now, *Doctor* Broadspeare, since we're being so formal about it, I know what you're going to say and I'm against it."

"But, Felix, we have to find out what's going on down there," Welsey chimed in.

"And get yourself killed! A flash flood could wash through there and take you know knows where? I've been doing a bit of research on my own, and there's no record of that cave. Do you expect me to stand by and let you go down there like Tom Sayer and Becky Thatcher with a couple of flashlights? You need more equipment than that, and I don't have it. Do you?"

Troy saw the sense in Amsdorfer's words. He hadn't intended on exploring unknown caves. All the work Keene and he did was in explored and well-mapped caverns and tombs. His stipend barely covered the hotel expenses, let alone foot the bill for a spelunking expedition.

"I can get it," said Welsey. "I can get everything we need."

Troy and Felix stopped glaring at each other and faced her.

"I said I can get everything we need. Ropes, lights, a generator—everything." She took a hard look at Felix and added, "You know I can."

"I know that, but just because you can doesn't mean that you should."

Troy stepped in between them and said, "What's going on? Am I missing something?"

Felix nudged him out of the way. "You stay out of this. You got her in enough trouble already."

"He's not getting me into trouble. I'll doing it on my own. Felix, we'll be back here the day after tomorrow, unless you want to arrest us for trespassing." She and Troy walked out of his house. Despite the curiosity gnawing away his insides, he knew better than to ask.

"Drop me off at the station," she ordered. "Then met me at Felix's the day after tomorrow. At dawn."

A rare, bright February sunrise found Troy standing next to Felix in the meadow by the stone with Skippy sniffing around the opening. Both men wore Carhartts, Troy's still creased from the store and Felix's stained and worn. The only sound was the low, continual groan of traffic moving on I-55 in the distance.

"You know they almost built the highway right over Monk's Mound?" said Felix, breaking the silence.

"No, I wasn't aware of that."

"My father headed the local committee that put a stop to it. My family's always loved this place. I hated to see those houses over there going in." He pointed to the south. "They bulldozed three mounds flat to put them in. I don't know why, but some people don't care for anything but making money. At least I can say this for you, Dr. Broadspeare, you don't seem like one of those."

"You can call me Troy, you know."

"I know. We'll see when all this is over. I think that's her now."

The sound of the Geo Tracker struggling against a load caught their attention. They saw the vehicle pulling a trailer loaded with gear. Crawling in first gear, she eased it across the frozen ruts with the trailer rocking from side to side.

"I told you I'd get it," she yelled from the open window. Felix guided her as close to the hole as possible. Troy recognized the equipment, the sort he had passed on highway work crews—large work lights, a generator, cans of gas, and an enormous winch bolted to the back of the trailer.

"And these too," she said, holding up a tangle of belts and webbing. "Swiss seats."

Troy raised an eyebrow.

"Don't tell me you've never heard of a Swiss seat? They're to lower us into the cave without breaking our necks."

"Where did you get all this?" Troy asked.

"I know somebody in the construction business. February is their slack time and they let me borrow it."

She pulled on the Swiss seat over her coveralls and helped Troy with his. When she put her arms around his waist to pull up on it to test is, Felix gave out a loud cough. She turned to him and said, "I've brought a third seat if you want to join us."

"Not me. Somebody's got to stay up here and mind the generator," he said, turning it on.

"Dr. Broadspeare," she said, turning her attention back to him, "hook this through that loop on the front." She handed him one of the cables attached to the winch. "Walk backwards towards the opening." The generator hummed, and he walked backwards, keeping the cable taut. He neared the edge of the hole and the ground suddenly gave way under his feet, letting him hang in mid-air.

"Are you okay?" she called down into the hole. He waved a thumbs up and she lowered him the rest of the way. Then she sent down the searchlights. While he was setting them up, she joined him.

"Where did you learn all this?"

"I told you, I know somebody in the construction trade. It sort of rubs off."

After the work lights were set facing the dark recesses of the cave, Troy reached out his hand and clasped hers. "For luck," he said. They turned on the lights and gasped.

The cave extended beyond the reach of the lights. The silt covering the floor sloped down ten feet before leveling off.

"Look," she said, pointing to an immense stone rising from the floor that had its top sheared off and then to the underside of the stone they found in the field. The same glyphs wound around it, breaking off as they reached to top. She added, "It's almost as if it were broken off and set in the ceiling."

"That's impossible," he replied. "I wonder what else is down here." They turned from the stone and saw pairs of shiny, obsidian columns rising from the floor at odd intervals. Each column bore glyphs like those on the stone.

"These have been knapped. Feel the edges."

Welsey ran a finger along the edge and jerked her and back—a drop of blood clung to the column, another dropped onto the floor. They walked from one set of columns to the other, kicking up the fine dust as they went. In the stillness of the cave, the dust rose up like a cloud around their feet.

"What could they be for?" asked Troy.

"Up near Monk's Mound, they had built a wooden version of Stonehenge to mark the equinox."

"That doesn't make sense down here in the dark."

"And those are in a circle. These form a line."

"Not a straight line. Those two are closer than these, and over there, a pair standing alone."

"A constellation?"

"We're underground. Hand me the lithographometer" He set it up at the base of the nearest pair, put on the headphones and adjusted the settings. "There's something here, Listen." He handed her the headphones. As she listened, she rhythmically swayed back and forth.

"You hear it, don't you?"

"It's familiar, but I can't place it."

"Damn, this is frustrating." He kicked the base of the column and the lithographometer shot out a piecing tone.

"This is exactly what happened before, in a cavern before the earthquake," he explained. He stepped back, looking down at the base of the columns. He began to hum, stopped, and listened. Very gently, the last note returned. He started to sing, "In a cavern, in a canyon…" and motioned for Welsey to join him, facing the columns. She followed his lead, increasing and decreasing tempo when he did, slowing down more and more until the words to Clementine were lost in the tones. He signaled a stop and the last note hung between the columns, almost visible in the rising dust cloud caught by the brightness of the work lights, dust motes vibrating between the columns.

"My God, they're not columns." He dropped to his knees, shoved the lithographometer out of the way, and dug into the silt with his bare hands. "Call down for a shovel. Make that two shovels." She ran back to the entrance and he continued to pull the silt away, careful not to touch the sharpened edges of the stone.

"Clear the dirt away from the base. It can't be that deep."

She joined him in digging, pulling shovelful after shovelful away. "I'm digging, but why?"

"They're not columns like we thought. See." He pointed into the hole they had dug and the revealed edges of the base. "The water washed all this silt down here and covered the bases. Look how they come together. And I'll bet that a little further down, we'll find a single, narrow column holding it up. Keep digging."

The dust cloud rose around them and despite their coughing, they kept on until they reached bedrock.

"Now what do you see?" Troy asked.

"It looks like one of your forks."

"Exactly, a tuning fork." He studied the other pairs of columns. "They're all tuning forks. But why?" He tapped the fork with the shovel handle. Nothing happened. He tapped is harder. Still nothing. He hauled back and gave it a good whack. They felt the earth vibrate beneath their feet. The screech from the lithographer pierced the air through the tiny headphone speakers. The ground continued to vibrate, knocking them off their feet into the dust. When it stopped, they looked into the freshly dug hole and saw a skull looking up at them. Troy pulled it from the silt. The back of it had been bashed in. In the space where it had been pulled out, another could be seen. This one led to two more, then three. All bore the same signs of ritual murder.

"I told you they practiced human sacrifice," she said.

"What sort of ritual could it have been with this collection of giant tuning forks laid out what looks like a random pattern?" He held the skull at arm's length as if it could tell him the answer. "Welsey, do you have the maps we've been working on?"

"Which one?"

"All of them."

She handed him the maps and held them up to the work lights and put one in front of the other with the light shining through. He gave them to her to hold and he took a step back for a longer view. He pointed to the columns they had dug out, to the map, then ran to another pair of columns and called out, "Point to the spot on the map, left of center, what do you see?"

"One of the clusters we'd charted."

He ran to a third column. "See where I am? How does it coordinate with the map?"

"Another cluster."

"And here?" he called from a fourth.

"The same." She dropped the map. "Are you telling me that these giant tuning forks match the linguistic clusters?"

"That's exactly it."

"But what about the fault line?"

He ran back to her, grabbed her by the hand and tugged her to a point between the nearest pair of columns. "It's right here, beneath our feet. It all makes sense now."

"What does?"

"Everything. How did the Cahokian priest-kings control the population? How did they get the tribes to move here, make their trade goods, and give themselves over for ritual sacrifices? How do you get them to build great mounds of dirt, so you can look down on the other tribes?" He spread his arms wide, "With this. This whole set-up controls the New Madrid Fault. They used this underground temple, this ritual space to move the subterranean stones at will, like they must have moved that stone we found in the field. To the locals they must have seemed like gods."

"That's crazy."

"Is it? Sing Clementine with me again, slowly and loudly."

They stood in the center and sang. When the tempo slowed, and the words disappeared, the floor vibrated like train was rolling by at high speed.

"You know what this means?" she said. "Not for the Cahokia Indians but for us, now. If you could . . ."

Before she could finish the cave went black. The droning of the generator stopped, and the dog began barking. They cried out for each other in the sudden darkness. Troy screamed in pain.

"Dr. Broadspeare . . . Troy, are you all right? Where are you?"

"I'm over here. I fell against the fork and gashed open my hand. I'm bleeding all over the place. Don't move, I'll come to you. Keep talking and I'll follow your voice."

A bright light suddenly stabbed the darkness, scanning the cave, searching until it shone on Welsey's face. Blinded, she put up her hand to shield her eyes.

"Don't move. Anyone," declared a bullhorned voice from the cave's entrance. A second light slashed through and settled on Broadspeare. "Stay right where you are, Dr. Broadspeare."

He jumped out of the light and a shot rang out, the sound echoing through the cave. The bullet struck the far wall with a pronounced "ping."

"Next time, Dr. Broadspeare, it won't be a warning. Don't move. We're coming down."

The work lights came back on and men in black uniforms rappelled into the cave, all of them armed.

"She's over there," said one of them.

"Get her and haul her out of here," said another.

"Mrs. Yergens, are you all right?" The speaker's voice was calm and professional, experienced in rescue operations.

"Why shouldn't I be?"

"Please don't run, Mrs. Yergens. We're here to help."

Troy spotted the guards approaching him with their weapons all pointing at him. "One move, Broadspeare, one move and that's it."

He stared down the muzzles of the AR-16s, motionless, feeling the blood drip off his hand going plop, plop in the silt.

"Do you see it?"

Even though one tried to keep him blinded with the glare of his flashlight, Troy saw the light of another searching the ground until it landed on the lithographometer.

"I think this is it, sir."

"Get it then. You, get Mrs. Yergens out of here immediately. And you, get Broadspeare while I keep him covered."

Troy saw them take Welsey while another headed to his machine. "Keep your hands off them!" He lunged at the guard and the shot reverberated off the cavern walls. Before he blacked out, Broadspeare heard Welsey call his name while they hoisted her out of the cave.

When he came to, he was still in the cave, but strapped to an emergency gurney cart.

"You're going to be fine, Broadspeare. If I wanted to kill you, I would have. I probably missed any major organs. A good dose of morphine will keep the edge of the pain off for now. And we bandaged up your hand, too. No charge. Men, get him out of here."

Troy felt the cart lift him off the ground and into daylight. The sun had passed the zenith and was approaching the horizon. They must have been down there most of the day.

Black vans with imposing SECURITY signs on the doors circled them, excepting for a single brown deputy sheriff's car supporting a bored deputy more interested in his smart phone than the events swirling around him. The deputy held open the front passenger door for Welsey when they marched her over to him and closed it behind her. A dark BMW slowly crawled over the rough meadow and stopped. Skippy ran from Amsdorfer, stood in front of the approaching car, barking. The car stopped and out of it stepped a man Troy wished he had never met before.

"Get that damned dog out of here before I kill it." Amsdorfer called the dog to his side and quieted him down. The man came over to Broadspeare, towering over the guards as they surrounded the gurney.

"So, you're Dr. Broadspeare," he said. "We've met before, remember?" He pointed to the BMW. "The shop did a real good job of patching up that mess you caused. I see you remember. I can tell by the bright spot in your eye. I used to see that on the line when the blocker saw it was me he had to block. The fear just took over."

"What…? Why…?" Troy slurred through the morphine taking effect.

The big man walked over the equipment trailer behind Welsey's Tracker. He tapped the side of it and said, "Next time you steal from somebody, you best watch out for who it belongs to before you act. It would be better for your health."

Through the morphine fog Troy read the sign: Blevins Construction. He was loaded into one of the black vans and passed out.

Chapter 6

He came to in a hospital surgery, with one bandage on his hand and another around his midsection like a mummy wrap. He tried to get up but both hands and feet were restrained.

"Shh. Don't move," said a whisper. He turned his head. Welsey sat in the chair by his head. "You're going to be fine. The bullet went straight through."

He turned his head back and looked around the room. It looked more like a clinic than a hospital. He tugged at the restraints, rattling the bed.

"Shh." She rested her hand on his arm. "Don't struggle. Try not to make any noise. We're going to try to get you out of here." She loosened the restraints, crossed the room and tapped on the door.

The door slowly opened and Felix pushed an empty gurney into the room. He motioned that they needed to hurry up. They eased Troy onto the cart and pushed it down the hallway, out the service door, and onto the loading dock. An old hearse sat in the bay with back door wide open. Troy tried to sit up, but Felix pushed him back down.

"Gently," whispered Welsey. Felix nodded and they slid the cart into the hearse. She closed the hearse door with barely a click, and she and Felix got into the passenger compartment, leaving the doors open. Without starting the engine, the hearse rolled slowly forward, the gravel crunching beneath the tires. "Good thing we're on a hill." Troy heard Felix whisper. At the bottom of the hill, he turned on the engine; they slammed the doors and pulled away from the clinic.

Looking through the back window, Troy saw a sign pointing to Blevins Urgent Care. *He's got his name on everything.*

The hearse hit a pot hole and Troy groaned.

"Felix, be careful."

"Yah, I'm doing the best I can. This thing hasn't been on the road for a long time. And in case you're wondering, Dr. Broadspeare, I got it cheap at an auction. Nobody else bid on it, imagine that. I thought it would be good for the farm. It was either this or the truck, and you've already had a ride in that. At least this time, you're dry."

"Thank you," said Troy. His voice sounded hollow inside his head. "Where are we going?"

"Someplace quiet and safe," Welsey replied. "Felix, take a right up ahead, through that gate.

Troy saw the ornate wrought iron gate pass by and wondered where he was being taken.

"This is some fancy place, he's got here. Are you sure it will be safe?" asked Felix.

"No one ever comes up here in February. Even in the summer he doesn't use it very much. Too busy with business, like he always is." An unfamiliar bitterness sharpened her comments. "Pull up to the garage, I've got an opener."

Why would she have an opener for this place? Troy wanted to ask but all his energy went into staying awake.

The garage door opened, and Felix pulled in the hearse and shut off the engine. The old hearse was conspicuously out of place next to the outline of a sports car nestled under a fitted tarp.

"Do you think you can walk?" she asked.

"I can try, but you both will have to help me." With Welsey on one side and Felix on the other, they made their way into the house. So, this is how the other half lives, Troy thought. Making their way through the kitchen and family room, he tried to focus on all the sports memorabilia. Several framed football jerseys hung on the wall along with poster sized team photos. The bookcase, carried trophies, not books. He wanted to stop and examine them, but his energy quickly drained away. "I need to lie down," he sighed.

Welsey took him down a hallway into a bedroom decked out with nautical gear. Felix balanced Troy while she pulled back the covers. After tucking him in, Felix said that he would give her lift to her Tracker on the way back to the farm. "And just to let you know, Dr. Broadspeare, I'm doing all this on account of her."

Time lost all meaning to Troy during his sleep. He vaguely remembered her coming in to check on him, giving him broth to drink, changing his bandages, and when the pain was too great, giving him a pill to quickly put him back to sleep. After what seemed to him like weeks, he said, "I'm hungry," and sat up in bed.

She told him he needed to get up and walk around, and that he should eat in the breakfast room. She helped him off the bed, balancing him as they walked through the house. When they entered the family room, he realized that this was a lake house for beyond the glass doors that took in the entire wall lay a lake, partially frozen, under the gray sky that drooped with the lingering days of winter. With her help, he made wide circles through the room, glancing at the photographs on the walls. A hockey team filled the first one. He stopped and studied it. There was something about the players in it that demanded his attention. He had seen some of these men before, but where? He leaned closer and would have toppled over is she hadn't caught him. He pointed to the picture. "Now I know. That man on the far right. He's the one who shot me. And that one next to him, he was there, too." He pulled away from her, used the back of the couch for balance, and went on to the next photo, one of a football team with all the players' signatures. A Super Bowl portrait of the team showed Blevins front and center. No one could mistake him, standing above all the rest. Troy studied the jerseys on the wall. Blevins name was on the back.

"Where the hell am I?" He lost his balance and toppled over. Welsey rushed to his side and gently pulled him from the floor and onto the couch. "Why the hell am I in Blevins' house? That SOB tried to kill me. Wesley, why have you brought me here, of all places? I thought I could trust you."

He glared at her, and she was no longer the young woman whose picture he had clutched the night Sarah left. He had trusted her before, believing what she had told him, believing what he had read about her. Maybe she was as fake as the last article he had written, filled with the gobbledygook of empty information. He looked at her and saw for the first time the reflection of Blevins in her nose, eyes, and chin.

"He's your father."

She gave a hint of a nod.

"And you're married."

She pursed her lips slightly and shook her head.

"In the cave they called you Mrs. Yergens."

With her lips still tight, she slipped a nod.

The room became warm, too warm, and the wound in his side throbbed. He breath went shallow.

"Tell me," he said through the shallow breaths, "the truth."

"Yes, Demetrius Blevins is my father." She took a framed photo from the back of the trophy shelf and handed it to him. Blevins dominated by sheer bulk. Standing next to him was the woman who gave Welsey her beauty and grace. Between them stood a little girl in overalls with her hair pulled into tight pigtails sticking up all over her head. The little ragamuffin she had mentioned before.

"This was the last picture of us as a family. My parents met while in college and got engaged when Dad was drafted for the pros. I guess she saw a bright future married to a football star, but it didn't turn out that way. She was from England…"

"I wondered where the British tone came into your accent."

"Yes. I loved the way she spoke. When I was little, and Dad was on the road with the team, she would read to me, and I would sit next to her on this enormous couch and listen. I didn't care what the story was about; I just wanted to hear the soft music of her voice."

"What happened then?"

"She grew tired of waiting for him to come home, tired of waiting for the off-season, tired of being the wife of a football superstar. One day, shortly after this picture was taken, she told me to pack, that we were going to England to visit her family. When I asked about Daddy, all she said was that he was off playing his game. That's what she called it 'his game.'"

"That explains the rest of your accent, the time in England. But not London."

"No. How do you know that?"

"Londoners have a different accent."

"If you think you're so clever, doctor of linguistics, tell me what happened next." She moved from the chair facing him to the couch where he sat.

"You moved back here, next to Felix. You and your mother returned, but she fell out of your life and Felix took her place. Your father took care of you during the off-season which included two, no, three extended vacations in northern Italy. Perhaps he had a job there. Am I close?"

She shivered. "That's scary. That's so close it's like you were living my life. Yes, Mom and I moved back at the court's insistence. She was never the same after that. You had already heard about how I wandered across the field to Felix's place. As far as northern Italy, Dad did some assistant coaching for the Milan Rhinos. I was thirteen and had the run of the city. I picked up some Italian that helped me when Felix taught me Latin."

He tried to shift towards her, but the bandage pulled against the wound causing him to grimace and groan.

"Troy?" She knelt beside him and checked the bandage.

"I'm all right. I must have shifted the wrong way. Come back up here and tell me some more. Tell me about your husband."

"He's dead."

"I'm sorry," said Troy with a sudden urge of apology.

"No need to be. As hard as it is to accept, I'm a widow. It sounds strange, doesn't it, being a widow before I'm thirty. I used to think of widows as old and gray." She paused and looked past him across the lake without looking at anything but the memory in her mind. She took a deep breath, the kind of breath taken before beginning a difficult chore.

"Are you sure you want to hear this?"

Troy said that he did and settled back into the couch.

"Danny—that was his name. Daniel Jose Yergens. Like me, he was mixed, only for him it was Mexican and White—Danish white. Maybe that's why we were drawn to each other. Neither of us fit into either culture. We met at the state park's museum one summer. Both of us had been hired as summer help. We were both in college and while I knew what I wanted to study, Danny was sort of lost. My father was dead set against our getting married, refusing to take part in the wedding. Felix gave me away, instead. I had hoped that Dad would have softened up after we had been married for a while. When Danny dropped out of school, my father gave him a job on one of his construction crews. Danny wasn't on the job more than month when the accident happened. At least they called it an accident."

She stopped, and again stared across the lake as if to gather her thoughts from the distant shore. "Those men that my father hire . . . some of them can be so rough. You met a few of the players from the hockey team he owns already, but that's their part-time job. Mainly, they run security."

"You don't think your father had anything to do with Danny's death, do you?"

"Not that anything can be proven. The inquest declared it an accident, but I was never convinced, especially when my father insisted I go back to finish my master's degree as well as that I stop using Danny's name. I refused to do both, if nothing else, to honor

Danny. For the past five years I've been known and Mrs. Yergens. Being a missus has a few advantages—it keeps the riff-raff away."

"That sounds well and good, but it doesn't explain everything." He sat up the best he could. If he had the strength, he would have gotten up and moved away from her before he continued. "It doesn't explain the deputy taking you away, and this place." He caught the room with a wave of his hand and tossed it into her lap.

"The deputy. Deputy Nuddley, our very own version of Barney Fife. My father had him there to make the raid look legal. Set a brown sheriff's department car in the middle of his black security vans and nobody pays attention. He hauled me off so you would think I was arrested, except he was too dumb to put me in the back seat. He brought me back to the radio station and dropped me off."

"That explains the deputy. What about this place."

"You already figured the owner out."

Troy gave a knowing uh-ha, followed with a weak smile.

"He doesn't know you're here. This is a summer cottage that gets used a few times a year, like the rest of the places around the lake. Who comes to a lake cottage in February? I figured this would be the last place he'd look."

"He's going to wonder what happened to me, especially since I disappeared from his clinic."

"He's not worried about that right now."

"How would you know, have you been talking with him? Been on the phone?"

"No, we're not that close. I still have a friend, one of Danny's old friends, on one of the construction crews. The one I borrowed the equipment from."

"An inside man."

"Sort of. The main thing is that he's not too worried about you, particularly now that he's got your . . . what did you call it?"

"A lithographometer. What in the world does he want with it? I was wondering why he was so interested in it. You don't think he has any idea what it's for, do you?"

"How could he? All I know is that some guy is supposed to come in and examine it, but this person won't be able to get here for three weeks."

"Do you have any idea who that might be?"

"No, except that he's done some sort of cyber-security work for my father before."

Troy attempted to stand but the shock of the pain sent him wobbling. Welsey jumped off the couch and caught him by the waist. "What's the matter, Troy?"

"I'm so damned tired of sitting here, that's all. How long is this going to take to heal, anyway?"

"I don't know, but they say that exercise helps the healing. Lean on me and we'll take a tour of the house."

While Troy struggled to trudge along, Welsey pointed out the billiard room, the wet bar, the multiple guest rooms, and the master suite. He couldn't image what it would be like to live in such luxury. "He's got a sauna, a hot tub, and a steam room," he exclaimed.

"Most of his friends are old NFL buddies and nearly all of them are in some kind of pain most of the time. Ever the good host, Dad keeps a supply of pain relievers on hand. I've had to give you a few of them, especially when we first brought you here."

After they arrived back to where they had started, she urged him to make another round. "This time, tell me about yourself. It only seems fair."

He told her about his father and mother and his education, but when he spoke of his wife and daughter, she paid fuller attention.

"And you've never seen your daughter? Not even a picture?"

He shook his head and said, "I didn't know she existed until she was two years old and my ex was getting married. The new husband wanted to adopt her. Their attorneys contacted me and I signed the papers. I still think it's for the best."

She said nothing and caressed his arm.

He shoved her hand away. "I didn't tell you that to gain your pity. Pity is the shallowest emotion around. It's the deeper ones that count. Those are the hardest to get. I'm tired and here's the door to my bedroom."

She helped him into bed, checked the dressing, and left. He thought he heard her whisper, "It isn't pity," but dismissed it as part of a dream.

One week later, Welsey told him that she had a surprise for him that she would show him after dinner. "That is, after you've made it four times around the house, stairs included."

"Are you sure you weren't training to be a physical therapist," he complained on the fourth round. She had her arm securely around his waist while he held on to her shoulder. He could have made it without her help, but never said so.

Dinner came from one of the gourmet restaurants that served the elite lake clientele. Welsey had picked up most of their other meals from the deli causing Troy to ask if she had ever learned to cook, to which she replied, no, for her studies had been far too important and most of the time, they had someone else to do the cooking. "The benefits of rich parents." Troy admitted the dinner was excellent, assuming this was the surprise she had talked about. He was wrong. The surprise came in a folder she handed to him.

"While you've been sleeping, I've been working. These are my notes and a report on what I've found so far, including everything that happened in the cave."

He opened the folder and skimmed the pages. "At first glance, this looks very thorough. Nice work with the appendices as well." He closed it, looked up at her, and said, "Are you telling me that it's time to get back to work?"

Before she could answer, he added, "I never bothered to thank you for everything. Until you came along, I had come to believe that all my theories were a bunch of hokum and that I was a fraud about to be caught."

"You don't need to thank me for anything. But I do have to say, Dr. Broadspeare, I've noticed a change. Something has happened to you since we came out of the cave.

"For the good, I hope." He reached across the folder and took her hand.

"Something very good."

"We've spent the last three days going over everything and something is still missing," he said, stretched out on the couch. Papers radiated around him like the rays from the sun. "And for the life of me, I can't figure it out. I feel it's right in front of me, looking at me, and grinning."

"Why don't we relax, watch TV, give our brains a rest."

He rose slowly, still tender from the wound, and went to the bookcase. "It still surprises me that here's an entire bookcase and not a single book. And all the videos are of football games. I hate football. So much for your TV suggestion."

Wesley came in, handed him the remote, and said, "find a channel." A buzzing came from her pocket. "The phone. Excuse me, I don't want any background noise that I might have to explain."

He sat back on the couch and surfed the channels. He had lost track of the days but the prevalence of religious and news programs informed him it must be Sunday morning. He stopped at an evangelist who paraded in front of an audience with a smile that looked like it was held on with Botox. He flipped to an interview of an unknown Deputy Secretary of State, then to the next, a Catholic Mass with the priest intoning the service, and onto a Lutheran service with the pastor looking like the priest, singing his part. He turned off the TV and glared at the screen. Suddenly he shouted, "Wait a minute" He turned the power back on and flipped through until he found the priest again. He leaned towards the screen and closed his eyes. Without opening his eyes, he flipped to the Lutheran service, still staring at the screen with his eyes closed. "Yes." He kept his eyes shut and swayed back and forth. "Yes, I know this. I know this."

The TV went off and when he opened his eyes, Wesley was standing directly in front of him.

"I know this," he said. "I know this." His face felt like it was shining.

"We have to get out of here.

Ignoring her, he continued to rock back and forth saying, "I know this."

"Troy!" she shouted. "Look at me. We have to get out of here now. And we have to make it look like no one was ever here. My father is coming tomorrow."

He shook his head as if waking. "What about your father?"

"He's coming here tomorrow. We have to make it look like we were never here and go."

"I thought you said he never comes up here during the winter."

"He never does. I don't know why he's coming now. But we have to clean the place and get out of here."

"And we have to find a church right away. Right now."

"Didn't you hear me?"

"Yes, your father is coming, we need to make it look like we were never here and leave. Yes, I get all that. But more important, we need to get to church before the end of the service."

"I don't get it."

"You will. Believe me, you will." He felt the radiance return to his face. She looked at him, confused. He grabbed her by the shoulders, held her, and said, "Welsey, it all makes sense, and we need to get to church so I can prove it to you. Where's the nearest Catholic Church. Orthodox would be better. Too bad it's not Saturday—then we could find a synagogue."

She took out her phone and looked for churches. She found seven. "I never knew there were so many. What kind do you want? The nearest is the Family Bible Church, KJV."

"King James Version. No, too modern. An older type."

"Older, how?"

"Older in the service."

"Here's a Catholic one. Close to it is an Episcopalian, and across the road from them is a Lutheran."

"The mother lode!" he screamed. "Let's go." He grabbed her by the arm and pulled her to the garage.

They got into the car, opened the garage door, and backed out. "What is this all about?"

"You'll see. What until you see it."

"When I said you had changed, I didn't think you had gone crazy."

"Drive faster, we need to get there on time."

She stepped on the gas and they sped through the town that was barely inhabited in the winter. She pulled up to the Catholic Church. Troy looked at the time for Mass on the signboard, and then his watch. "Perfect. Come on."

He pulled her by the hand, rushed past the usher who stood holding out a bulletin as they went by. Troy worked his way to a back pew and sat down. He clasped his hands in his lap, bowed his head, and closed his eyes.

"Are you praying?" she whispered in his ear.

"No. Close your eyes. Blot out the sounds and feel the pulse, the rhythm." He started rocking as he had on the couch. She followed his directions and moved with him. The others in the pew shifted away from them. Soon the usher stood by them and tapped Troy on the shoulder.

"Sir," whispered the usher, "is there anything we can do for you?"

Troy raised his head and whispered back, "No, thank you." He shook Wesley, pulled her up by the hand and left the church.

"Where's the Episcopalian?"

She looked at her phone. "Half a block this way."

"We'll walk." His brisk pace quickly slowed and he clutched his hand to his side. "I'll be fine. First the church."

They went in as before and repeated what they did in the Catholic Church. As Troy rocked, he felt the change in Wesley's swaying.

"Troy, if feels like . . . but it can't be."

"Time for one more. The Lutheran. Go get the car and I'll meet you across the street."

"Shouldn't we go home?"

"No. Not now. We're too damn close."

"Don't swear in church."

They entered the Lutheran Church minutes before the pastor finished his sermon. Several members glared at them for arriving so late. Without being able to find an empty pew in the back, they had to sit in the unoccupied middle. Again they hunched over, hands clasped, eyes closed while the service spun on around them. They rocked slowly back and forth. Troy began to hum, very quietly and very slowly. Welsey picked up on it and hummed in reply.

"Excuse me, sir, madam." The usher was leaning over them. "This is no place to sing 'Clementine.' I'll have to ask you to leave." Troy nodded in agreement and they filed out of the church into the parking lot. Welsey shined.

"You got it, didn't you? It's the ritual that moves the stones. Not only the frequencies of the tones but the ritual, the deep and ancient ritual that is as old as the stones themselves. That's what we need."

Wesley smiled and said, "Yes, I understand it all now, but this isn't the time to debate theories. If my father finds out that we've been hiding out in his precious summer cottage, right under his nose, who knows what kind of fit he's going to throw? We've got to make it look like we were never near the place and get out as fast as we can."

"Once we're out of there, we'll go back to the radio station and listen to the tapes again. Now that we know what to look for, maybe we can reassemble the ritual." His smile collapsed into a scowl. "There's an enormous problem. Suppose we recreate the ritual. How will we test it? When Felix called to check on us, he said that something else going on with the cave. And your father still has my lithographometer. Why, I don't know. And to make matters worse, I'm starting to ooze." He pulled back his coat and lifted his shirt. A damp, pink spot spread over the bandage.

"Lean on me," she said, "I'll take care of you."

Once they were back in the house, she removed the dressing to reveal that it wasn't as bad as they had thought. With a new bandage, he insisted that he help clean. "You've done so much for me already, it's the least I can do," he said.

"And run the risk of you tearing yourself open over a bag of trash? Just stay on the couch out of my way. We need to get out of here long before he shows up."

As soon as these words left her mouth, they heard the sound of the garage door rising. They looked at each other in shock with the expression of "now what" reverberating off the walls.

"I need to hide," he said.

"What will I tell him?"

"Tell him that you needed the cottage to recover from the trauma of the cave."

"He'll never believe that," she said while helping him into the closet.

"Why not? You're his daughter."

The door to the garage opened and Blevins' voice echoed through the house. "Welsey! I know that's your car's here, but where are you?"

"I'm right here, Dad."

"What are you doing here? You haven't been up here in years."

"You always said I could use it anytime I wanted to. You even gave me the key and the garage door opener, don't you remember? After what happened, I wanted to get away, to find someplace quiet where I could think."

He snorted and said, "Well, you're going to have company now."

From inside the closet, Troy heard another set of footsteps.

"Put it on the table," Blevins ordered. "I wasn't expecting anybody to be up here, so it looks like I'll have to introduce you. Wyatt Dobrinski, this is my daughter, Welsey Yergens. Welsey, Wyatt."

"Nice to meet you, Ms. Yergens."

"It's missus."

"Sorry." He turned his back to her and said, "Now, Mr. Blevins, you called me here for a job and I want to get on with it. I need to be in Washington early tomorrow."

That voice. Troy recognized it, but the Polish last name didn't match the accent. No hint of Eastern Europe. The nasal quality. The swallowed consonants. It's the fabricator. What is he doing here? Standing in the closet weakened him, causing his knees to buckle. He reached up for the closet bar only to grab a flimsy hanger. He toppled against the door and fell into the room.

"Why Dr. Broadspeare," said Blevins. "I'd have thought you would have gotten some sense pumped into you. You should have run off after your self-dismissal from the clinic. Here, let me help you off the floor."

Blevins reached down and with one arm pulled from the floor as if he were picking up a crumpled coat. "Let me dust you off," He punched him in the wound. Broadspeare groaned and doubled over. Welsey rushed over only to be stopped by Blevins' outstretched palm. "You stay out of this, young lady. You don't know what you've gotten yourself into, and if I have to get you out of this, I'm going to do it my way."

"Do you mean like you did before with Danny?" Her words came out like acid.

Blevins smiled and said, "If you want to think it that way." He turned his attention to Broadspeare. "I believe you would be more comfortable sitting down, Professor." He tossed Troy into an armchair and told Welsey to sit down in the opposite chair.

"I'd introduce you two, but I know you've already met." Blevins said, nodding between Broadspeare and Dobrinski. Dobrinski looked at Broadspeare, his face empty of emotions. "My work goes to the highest bidder," he said, "and Mr. Blevins has been paying very well for specialized work long before you showed up, Dr. Broadspeare. You were just a side line—pocket change."

"Open it up." Blevins pointed to the lithographometer.

Dobrinski ran his hands over the aluminum cover. "You've been a bit rough on it, Dr. Broadspeare. Good thing I made it built to last." He opened the case and blew dust off the surface.

"Blevins, what do you want with it? It's a highly specialized scientific instrument that won't do you any good," Troy said.

"I beg to differ with you, Professor. I know exactly what this is for. It's not all that different from a seismograph. I'm not some dumb jock; I know about seismographs. I also know about earthquakes and what they can do." Blevins strode across the room and took a position in front of the glass doors. "I grew up in East St. Louis. It doesn't look much better now than when I was a kid. It was the poor cousin to the big city across the river. But I had two things going for me—bulk and brains. Everybody knew the bulk, but they didn't know the brains. I used my bulk to train my brains. Got me into college. Put me in the NFL. Made me a whole lot of money, like a few other black men. I saw what happened to the ones without the brains, I wasn't going to be one of them. I invested in land, and that led to constructing buildings on the land. This made me more money than football ever did. There's one problem, however, with investing in land. There's just so much of it, and somebody has already taken the best locations and built on it. And location, as everyone says, is everything."

"How does your life story have anything to do with me and my work," Troy asked.

"It would have been none at all until I got a call from our mutual friend here." He indicated Dobrinski with a brush of his hand. "He's done some particularly discrete work for me that needn't be discussed, and he keeps an eye open for the unusual. When you gave him the design for your device, he told me about it. Then when my daughter emailed you . . ."

"Dad, don't tell me that . . . "

". . . that what? That a father's been looking out for his daughter? I didn't think anything of it at the time, just you and your hobby going on in that old radio station of mine."

"So, that's how somebody broke in without leaving a trace." Troy said.

"I was hoping to put a little scare into you."

"That still doesn't explain very much," Troy added.

"No, it doesn't, that is, until I started putting things together. I said I got brains. My brain looked at the data. I need vacant land on which to build. Some professor has a device that has something to do with seismic action. My daughter is up to her ears in old radio shows, playing them at very slow speeds."

"You've been stalking me!" exclaimed Wesley, jumping to her feet.

"Only out of fatherly concern."

She snarled at him and turned towards the trophy case.

"She's told you about the New Madrid Fault, didn't she?" Without waiting for Troy to reply, Blevins continued, "In real estate there's a legal device called first options, that if someone wants to sell, I get the first option to buy. Most folks don't think an earthquake will ever hit here; after all, this isn't San Francisco."

"But if an earthquake should happen," Troy offered.

"Ah, the professor is using his brains now. If an earthquake would happen, one of those once in a hundred years, maybe a thousand years earthquake, there'd be a whole lot of land available. Not to speak of the amount of rebuilding that would have to take place."

"And if you knew when one might happen."

"Not 'might,' Professor, but when and how. My men gave me a full report of what went on down in that cave."

Troy noticed Welsey pick up the heaviest trophy. He stood up took a step toward Blevins. "Do you think, Blevins, that I'm going to help you, then you're mistaken. You might know what happened down there, but that's only one piece of the puzzle."

Blevins threw back his head and laughed. He pointed to Dobrinski and motioned with his finger to push something. Dobrinski took out his smart phone, tapped it, and the lithographometer began to sing, "In a cavern …" Blevins, still laughing, said, "There's an app for that. I had Dobrinski install a hidden recording chip. I didn't know what you and Welsey were up to and I had to know. Now, I know your little secret about the Cahokia Indians, and I'm …"

Before he could finish, Welsey smashed his head with the trophy. "I hate you. You've never been a father to me."

"Let's get out of here," Troy said. "Grab the lithographometer."

Welsey reached for it but stopped when she saw the gun Dobrinski pointed at her. "I can't let you just take it. If you want it, I need $9,750 cash, right now."

"We don't have that kind of money, and I already paid for it once."

"He already paid for it twice," said Dobrinski waving the gun towards Blevins who groaned. Again, as emotionless as a computer voice, he said, "Cash. Take it or leave it."

Blevins groaned, leaned up on one elbow, and slumped back onto the floor.

"We'll leave it," said Troy. Dobrinski shrugged his shoulders and lowered the gun.

Troy grabbed Welsey's arm and tugged her towards the door. As he groaned with every step, they dashed the best they could into the garage, into her Tracker, backing out of the driveway past a black security van. Troy looked over and saw the man who had shot him sitting in the van's driver's seat watching them leave.

"What do you think they're going to do?" asked Troy.

"I think they're going to come after us," said Wesley, looking in the rear-view mirror.

She hit the gas and drove as fast as she could through the tight turns of the shoreline road, flying past mansions, past trailer parks, and through the town that was deserted of summer visitors. The drive whipped Troy from side to side and every time he crashed into the door, he groaned.

"I'm sorry," she said.

"Drive. Don't worry about me. We've got to get away from them. Is there any other place we could go?"

She turned into a public park and wove through curves like a gymkhana driver. Troy clung to the shoulder strap. He looked behind them and saw the van right behind them, keeping a static distance. "Why aren't they gaining on us? Maybe they just want to tail us," he said.

"Let them tail this." She turned the Tracker towards the beach. The park sat on the crest of a high hill overlooking the beach with a steep slope descending onto the sand. She drove the front end of the car to the crest of the hill, and they dropped, careening down the hill.

"Hold on," she yelled.

The black van stopped at the top of the hill for a moment and then plunged over, slipping and turning sideways. It leaned on two wheels and was about to flip over when it righted itself on the beach.

Welsey dropped it into four-wheel drive and rutted a way through the muddy beach towards the lake. The van slogged around in the mud, got a grip, and creeped after them, avoiding getting stuck.

"That didn't work," she said. "One more place to go." She drove onto the ice. "Let's see what they're made of."

The van hesitated and then pulled onto the ice after them. Welsey hugged the shore line where the ice as thicker.

"Do you see any sign of a boat ramp?"

"Yes, over there." Troy pointed past a large three story beach house lined with balconies. The slush of the ice slopped through the holes in the floor. The van shortened the distance between them.

"They're trying to catch us now," he said.

"The ice looks thinner over there," she said and pointed the Tracker in that direction. She gripped the wheel for all its worth and pushed on the gas. The vehicle wanted to slide to the left and then to the right, but she wouldn't let it. He looked out the window and saw the open water of the middle of the lake getting closer and closer.

"We're almost there," she said. "Grab onto something—now!" She twisted the steering wheel sharply to the right, and they spun across the ice toward the open water. The ice cracked under the weight. She slammed on the brakes, locking the wheels, and they were nearly on top of the water. She rammed the gearshift into reverse, released the brake, and gave it the gas. The wheels spun against the ice fighting for traction. The van tried to follow but slid out of control. The passenger door flew open to reveal the guard frantically fighting against the safety belt and the driver screaming at him. The Tracker's tires finally bit into the ice and they backed away from the open water. The van stopped close to where the Tracker had been. The sound of cracking ice shattered the air and the van went down.

Welsey drove slowly to the boat ramp and pulled off the lake. Troy looked back to see the two guards struggling onto the ice.

"Don't worry about them. They're ex-SEALs or something. My father makes sure of that."

"We need a better place to stay. And we need those tapes from the radio station. Go to the station first. Let's hope that in all the confusion they haven't set a guard over it. Then we'll worry about the place.

The radio station was as they had left it. They grabbed the most important tapes and equipment and packed it into the Tracker with barely enough room for Welsey and Troy.

"We need a place that's quiet, without a lot of background noise," he said. "A place where nobody will notice us and what we are doing. A house, or a hotel, or an office, an apartment—a place where your father isn't known—or from someone who doesn't like him, a rival. I'm sure he's stepped on more than a few toes in this area. Who's his biggest competitor?"

"That would be Joe Larcher, I think. But we've never met."

"All the better. Let's find his office."

Larcher's office was in the former Union Station converted to an upscale office complex. Welsey pulled into the parking lot, her trashed out Tracker overflowing with goods making a sharp contrast to the Audis and Volvos parked in the lot.

"What are you going to tell him?" she asked as they approached the tall doors of bronze glass and polished brass handles.

"I don't know yet. Maybe the truth, but I doubt if he'd believe it."

They stepped inside, and the receptionist stopped them. She was about Welsey's age and doing her best to look clean and professional. Troy introduced himself as Dr. Broadspeare and Welsey as Mrs. Yeager, and no, they didn't have an appointment, but they urgently needed to see Mr. Larcher.

"I'm sorry, but if you have to have an appointment."

"Tell him right now that if wants to beat Blevins at his own game, really beat him, he needs to give us fifteen minutes. That all we need. Fifteen minutes."

After the receptionist disappeared down the hallway, Troy leaned over and whispered, "I hope I can last fifteen minutes. That ride made it worse." He pulled his hand from under his shirt, the palm glistening with the blood seeping through the bandage.

Welsey was about to answer when the clicking of the receptionist's heels stopped her. Behind the receptionist followed Larcher. He was in his sixties, with a gray balding head and deep sag lines etching his face. His belly hung over his cinched belt. "So, you're a doctor," he said.

"A PhD, not a medical doctor. Dr. Troy Broadspeare." They shook hands.

"Yergens, Welsey Yergens."

Larcher shook her hand, but instead of releasing it right away said, "You look familiar. We've met somewhere before." He furrowed his brow and continued to grip her hand. "Now I remember." He clasped her hand with both of his and gave a grandfatherly shake. "You're Blevins' daughter. I'll bet you don't remember me."

She shook her head and retrieved her hand.

"Your father came to me after he retired from football, wanting to invest in real estate. I told him it was a good idea. If I had any idea what kind of double-dealer he would turn out to be, I would have sent him packing. I guess I was overwhelmed by that Super Bowl ring and all. Now, why would his own daughter want to get at him? Come back in my office. You've got fifteen minutes."

Broadspeare told him everything and the old man sat behind his desk shaking his head in disbelief and finally saying, "That's the craziest thing I've ever heard and either you're telling the truth, or I'm setting myself up for the wildest con game since Satan conned Eve. I'll go along with you. It won't cost me much and if it gets at Blevins, it's worth it. I've an old property that I think would fit. It's an old church building out in the country. I keep the power on to maintain it, so you might as well use it for a while. Rachel will give you the key and directions to the place.

They followed the directions and discovered that the setting was perfect, about five miles from Cahokia

State Park. The old church had a small apartment attached for the visiting preacher. The sanctuary was bare since the members had sold off the pews years before to antique collectors to raise enough money to keep the church in operation for an additional year. Time and cultural change had taken their toll, and for the past three years, the building was up for sale—too big for a regular house, too small and out of the way for a church or store.

By the time they found it, Troy was tightly holding his side. His bandage needed to be changed and he knew it, occasionally glancing at the stain that had spread through his shirt onto his coat. When they were inside, they turned up the heat and found the apartment.

Larcher staged the apartment with sufficient furniture to give an air of hominess. The single bedroom had a double bed, a dresser, and nothing else. The combined living and dining room held a dinette and a couch. The kitchen was sparingly stocked with a few pots and dishes. Troy stumbled into the bedroom and collapsed on the bed. As his dressing was changed, they realized that the appearance was worse than the damage and more energy had been drained than blood. As he lay in the bed, guilt crashed upon him in waves as her listened to Welsey unloading the Tracker. *I should have been there for her.*

"I'm sorry," were the first words out of his mouth when he came to, and she was sitting on the edge of the bed.

"For what?"

"For being such a useless lump." He raised his arms into the air and let them collapse onto the bed.

"You've no reason to be. This has been a real eye-opening experience."

"Why do you say that?"

"For one, I learned that crack-pot ideas are often the best, and two, I never would have found out the truth about how ruthless my father truly is."

"I'm thankful for the first and sorry for the second."

"Like I said, you needn't be sorry. He and I were never that close. I knew more about him than I knew him. He was more of a presence and a name than a father. Felix was more of a father to me. I tried to give him a pet name, like Popsie, but he would never let me. Felix—that's all he would allow. Speaking of him, I should give him a call. You rest."

Chapter 7

Troy fell asleep and rituals haunted his dreams, images of priests and choirs and songs, voices chanting ancient words without meaning that pulsed through the ages in the solemn counting of eons. Dreams that took him farther and farther back, as if he were living in them. He wandered among a forest of tuning forks, vibrating the droning note against a background of melody barely heard. He reached out to touch, but his hand began to bleed and the hole in his side opened, like a mouth, and chanted in that achingly familiar, but uncommon way that he had heard in the church in Hermann, in the churches in Bellville, in the caves and caverns. Then the bed began to shake, echoing the pattern. He tried to call out, but his throat only croaked. He tried to yell and felt his body shutter.

"Troy! Troy! What's happening?" It was Welsey. She stood by the side of the bed. He reached out and took her hand. She sat down beside him. "You were calling out, but in some strange way. I was setting up the equipment when I heard you. I recorded some of it on my phone."

"Play it back."

She did so. He asked her to play it a second time. "I've heard this before. It's like the ritual is inside me. Maybe it's because we're staying in a church. Maybe because I was delirious. It's one more bit to work with. Help me sit up."

She plumped up the pillows for him and shifted him in the bed. "I spoke with Felix. He says that something strange is going on down in the cave. He doesn't want to go near it, but he can hear noises coming from it, and at night light shines out of it."

"I have an idea what your father is doing down there, but we need to test it out first. We're going to need some extra equipment like a big wash tub, some sand—enough sand to cover the bottom of the tub by a couple of inches—and a big flat rock. If you can get that, I think I should be able to set the rest of it up."

During the time she was gone, Troy continued working in the old sanctuary, now a large bare room stripped of all church furniture except for a faded mural above the choir loft that looked like the page taken from a medieval psalter. He had brought in a table and chair and here he sat, listening to the archived recordings. When she returned, all his tuning forks lay on the table and beside each fork was a card referencing one of the recordings. The moment he heard her enter the church, he called for her to hurry to him.

"Welsey, We've been going at this in the wrong way. I finally figured it out. Keene was wrong. Not completely, but mostly."

"Do you mean that all his work was meaningless?"

"Not meaningless, only headed in the wrong direction. He was looking for vocal patterns in the movements of the rocks, specific vocal patterns."

"But that's what we've been doing."

"And that's what's been leading us off the right trail. We've been close the whole time, so close we should have seen it but we were blinded by what we were expecting to find."

"If it's not the vocal patterns, then what is it?"

"Something deeper than the vocal patterns. What are vocal patterns made of?"

"Vibrations."

"Exactly. Before you can have vocal patterns, you have vibrations. But what if the vibrations don't end up as vocalizations?"

"If they're not vocalizations, then…" She paused and he watched her thinking it through for herself. He fought the urge to tell her the answer. She had been with him through this journey and to tell her would destroy the joy of discovery. ". . . If not vocalizations, then some other form of vibrations, like . . ." His heart beat faster while saw the realization brighten her face. ". . . like music, like the music we heard in the churches."

"Yes, like the music they used to sing here, up there." He pointed to the choir loft and stood up. He stared at the mural. Without taking his eyes off it he walked up the stairs to the loft, all the time saying, "Yes, the music, the ritual music that predates vocalization. Keene hadn't gone back far enough to make the primeval connection." He stopped when he got to the faded mural.

"Welsey, do you see that piece of paper that looks like strange music? It's a copy of a chart Keene had hidden in the fork-case. This is remarkable." She found it, brought it up to him, and held it by the mural.

"They're the same with four lines and shaped notes," she said.

"Nashure," Troy called out as if to the heavens. "You were so close, so incredibly close. If only you had pushed on to the next step and payed closer attention to the changes in the vibrations and not the sounds. Now it is finally making sense." He took Welsey by the hand and pulled her quickly down the stairs to the main floor. "I have to show you what I've been doing. I followed the changes in tones we noted earlier and set the fork that most closely matched the tonal shift.

That's what's on the table. Then I took those shifts, extracted the tones from the recordings and reassembled them here." He pointed to a file on the computer's screen. "Listen." He clicked on the file and a modulating tone came from the speakers. "And when I slowed it down …." He moved the mouse and clicked.

"That's the same sound that we heard in the church services."

"Exactly. But now comes a new question, how does this fit with what happened in the cave? Time to test the hypothesis. We'll set the experiment over here." He grabbed the tub's handle and dragged it to the center of the sanctuary. "Now the stone and the sand."

"I'll get those," she said. I don't want you to start bleeding again." She laid the stone in the bottom of the tub and poured sand over it to the depth of two inches.

"This is the cave floor," he said. "Place the forks according their placement in the cave. She followed the map and set the forks to match the pattern they had found.

"Let's see what happens when we add the tones." He programmed the file to play on a continuous loop and turned it on. They leaned over the tub, their heads close to each other, and watched. The forks vibrated, and the vibrations sent waves out through the sand, the ripples coming off each fork meeting and combining.

She turned her head and whispered into his ear, "Turn it up."

He did, and the vibrations became more intense. They leaned closer, their cheeks almost touching. He felt the softness, the lamb's wool softness of her hair against his ear. He lay his hand over hers and their fingers entwined.

"Welsey." Her name slipped from his lips. She turned her head and their lips were about to touch when the tub started to vibrate wildly, the sand jumping chaotically, and a loud crack rebounded off the sanctuary walls. Inside the tub the forks lay scattered on the sand and the stone had shifted out of the sand, broken into three pieces.

"Oh my God," he said. "This is more than ever imagined. I don't think your father has any idea of what he's messing with. If only he still didn't have the lithographometer."

"Why is that important? Look what we did without it." She pointed at the disarray in the tub.

"We caused that because we knew what we were looking for along with the materials to put the recording of the ritual together. That's what the lithographometer would be able to do when Dobrinski figures it all out."

"But will it end up like this?" Again she pointed to the tub.

"If it isn't carefully controlled it will. The whole Mississippi River valley—St. Louis, New Orleans, Minneapolis, Chicago—you name it. If it's between the Appalachians and the Rockies, who knows what would happen."

"But according to what you said before, the Cahokia priest-kings knew how to control the shock waves. We don't."

"We're still missing something. If I had the lithographometer, I'd have a good chance at figuring it all out, but your father has it, and we need to get it from him before it's too late."

Her cell rang. It was from Amsdorfer. "Felix, what's going on?"

"Is that Dr. Broadspeare there?"

"Yes."

"Put it on the speaker phone. Dr. Broadspeare, you need to hear this, too. Things are starting to heat up around here and I don't like it one bit. I've had to run some of Blevins' men off my property. Good thing they didn't know the gun was empty. I'm standing by the hole, as close to the stone as I want to get. I'm going to point the phone to the hole. You should be able to hear this. Skippy, be quiet."

Over the speaker Troy and Welsey heard the grinding of machinery, the dull and solemn grunting of workers, and an ominous, hollow sound.

"Mr. Amsdorfer," Troy said, "can you see what's going on?"

"I'm not that close. I can see the light coming out of the hole, it's a lot brighter than before, and a lot of shadows moving in front of the lights. It reminds me of a mineshaft or something. I'm going to try to get a bit closer."

They heard him grunt and comment that he was getting too old to be crawling on the ground.

"I'm here. I can barely see in. They got plenty of lights down there, and … oh my gosh, they got one of them little Bobcats down there moving the silt all over the place. Let me edge a little bit more."

"Felix, stop. You don't have to do this," whispered Welsey.

"I'll be careful. Just a bit more…" The cell's speaker emitted Skippy's barking followed by a thudding noise and an angry voice, then the metallic click of guns being locked and loaded. The phone went dead.

Welsey tried to call but only got the message that the voicemail account had never been set up. "I was going to do that for him," she said, putting the phone away.

"We've got to get back there right away, but how?" he said. We can't go in the same way as before. How did they get in? How did they get a Bobcat down there?" We didn't explore the whole cave; we only saw one part of it. Where could the entrance be? Where's the map?"

She took out the maps they had created, along with all the others they had collected—topographical, historical, aerial, road, archeological and others. "Which one?"

"All of them." He lay them out on the sanctuary floor. "Here's the entrance on Felix's farm." He drew a circle around it. "Here's the highways. Here's the layout of the mounds both inside and outside the park. Here's that strip of ground by the park that your father wants to turn into a shopping center."

"It's right next to the park."

"Take a closer look. Part of it is on park property. Where's the satellite shot?"

"If we had internet out here, I could use the computer. The phone will have to do. Google satellite." She handed him her smart phone.

He expanded the image and said, "The property line on the plat map lies here." He squinted and looked at the phone. "And here's a building that sits mostly on the shopping center's ground."

"You said, 'mostly.'"

"This is an obvious encroachment on state property. Do you have any idea what might be in that building?"

"I stopped paying attention to Dad's business a long time ago. Somebody in the park office certainly would have noticed. Somebody like Evelyn Tolkens." When she mentioned Token's name, Welsey stiffened up.

"You used to work for her, didn't you?"

"During the summers, and they were the worst I ever spent. That woman doesn't know a thing about the mounds or the Indians except for what's in the tourist guide. The only reason she keeps her job is her connections."

"Connections to your father."

"You don't think that this construction site masks a way in, do you?"

"There's only one way to find out. Let's go, but drive carefully. I'm still very sore."

Troy grabbed the tuning forks while Welsey gathered up flashlights.

A tall chain-link fence topped with concertina wire encircled the construction site for the shopping center. Across the front of the gate stretched the sign: Coming Soon Cahokia Mounds Mall.

"Isn't it a bit odd that a construction site would have razor wire at the top? One touch of that and you've got a nasty gash. Barbed wire, maybe, but not that stuff," Troy said, pointing his light to the top of the fence. They walked around the perimeter getting as close to the construction shed as possible. "Listen." They stopped and cocked their ears towards the shed, hearing a low, intermittent rumbling. "Do you know what a Bobcat sounds like?" he asked.

"Probably that. This must be how they got down into the cave. This isn't a shed, it's an entrance."

"And this place's been built within the last week. Look at the fence posts." Around the base of the fence posts lay piles of fresh dirt.

"We've got to get in there, but if we get past the fence, there's the lock on the door." He shone his light on the shed revealing a large, hardened padlock in the door's hasp.

"Troy, this doesn't make sense. The fence is locked from the outside with a chain and padlock. The door to the shed is locked from the outside with a padlock, and Felix has been watching the hole in the meadow."

They looked at each other and simultaneously exclaimed, "There must be a third way in!"

"This is for the equipment, like that Bobcat. The other must be for the people. Now where might that one be?" Troy asked.

"When I worked at the park I remember Tolkens being slipshod about most things except for the gift shop and an area off Woodhenge that was roped off and blocked by a sign explaining it was closed due to an ongoing archeological dig. I never saw anyone going there. Then a door was placed over it and I didn't think any more about it. That could be it."

Woodhenge, the ancient Cahokian version of Stonehenge built with enormous tree trunks instead of standing stones, lay on the far edge of the park in the shadow of Monk's Mound. Between Troy and Welsey lay the open ground of ancient Cahokia. They turned off their flashlights and made their way using the shadows of the smaller mounds to mask their way. No one should be there, but no sense taking chances. The acrid smell of cigarette smoke stopped them before they reached Woodhenge.

They crept on, slowly, stopping in the shadows and listening, making sure they weren't noticed. The door to the "dig" was opened and light shone from the depths, casting the silhouette of the smoker into the night. The smoker turned. There was no mistaking the taut figure of Evelyn Tolkens. Broadspeare took the thick fountain pen from his pocket, creeped up behind her, clamped his hand over her mouth, and jabbed the pen into her back.

"Not a sound, Ms. Tolkens. Not a sound." Welsey's eyes widened in disbelief. "Do you think we should tie her up and leave her out here?" he asked.

Wesley mouthed, "We have no rope."

"We'd better bring her along in case she screams or does something foolish." He pushed the pen into her ribs. "Not a sound. And don't turn around either. Just take us in. Got it? Nod your head if you agree."

She nodded.

With Tolkens in the lead, they walked down the slope into the cave. The floor had been cleared of silt and they walked on bare rock. Blevins had turned the cave into a regular construction site with timbers shoring up the walls and lights strung along the cave walls illuminating the glyphs carved into the stone. Troy longed to study the markings. If only I didn't have to keep my eyes on her, he thought.

"Your father must have quite the work crew to get all this done is such a short time."

"That's how he got to be first in the business," she said with a hint of daughterly pride. "If only he hadn't been such a beast in other ways."

The Bobcat had pushed most of the silt away from the bases of the forks and the rest was being cleared away by the workers with shovels and brooms. Two men stood guard over Felix who tried to stand when he saw Welsey and Troy. They pushed him down onto the ground. "Stay put, old man."

"Mr. Blevins, we've got company."

Blevins looked up from his work with Dobrinski and the lithographometer to see the parade led by Tolkens.

"Dr. Broadspeare. I'm glad you're here. It saves me the trouble of hunting you down. And you brought my loving daughter. I still have that little present you gave me last time, dear." He rubbed the back of his head.

"Dimitri, watch out, he's got a gun," cried Tolkens. She ran to Blevins and hid behind him. Without a move from Blevins, three security guards rushed at Troy and Welsey, snapping the pen out of his hand. The guard held it up and the chrome clip flashed in the light.

Blevins pushed Tolkens out of the way and snarled at her, "It was a pen. He fooled you with a damned pen. You really are as dumb as they say. Get out of the way and watch the show."

She slipped away, sulking.

"Blevins, if you stop now, pull out all your equipment and your men and leave my lithographometer, you'll be a hero. You can have the credit for finding the greatest discovery of pre-Columbian history in North America, maybe all of the Americas."

"I've already got a belly full of fame, Broadspeare. You saw my wall of trophies, and that's not counting the ones in storage. I'm after the money, pure and simple. Nobody can eat fame."

"And I won't press charges."

"Charges? There won't be any charges. In one version of the deputy's report you died in an accident when you first tried to get into this cave."

"What do you mean, 'one version'?"

"The one that has me and my crew coming to your rescue after you fell down this hole in Amsdorfer's meadow." The grin that spread across Blevins' face matched the dismay in Broadspeare's. Blevins' laughter rattled through the cave, setting one of the smaller forks vibrating. "Too bad your body was never recovered." Blevins ordered his guards to keep an eye on him, this time to shoot to kill. He crossed over to Dobrinski who ignored everything except the lithographometer.

"It's ready," said Dobrinski, "Ready for exactly what, I don't know, but it's ready. I've reversed it so the signal goes out and not in."

Keeping his eyes on the guards, Troy took a tentative step toward Dobrinski and Blevins. "Wait! You don't have the whole picture. We tested this out and the trial run got out of control. You'll rip open the entire Mississippi River valley."

"Don't be ridiculous," said Blevins. "All we're going to do is sent a little shock wave through western Illinois. It won't do much more than knock down a few old buildings that need to come down and be rebuilt. Dobrinski, go ahead."

Dobrinski turned knobs, flipped switches and swiped his hand across the screen. The vibrations Broadspeare had recorded echoes out from the speakers set up around the cave. Faint vibrations slithered through the floor of the cavern and into the forks. The forks echoed in reply, one responding to the other in tones so low that they couldn't be heard, only felt in the chest, in the lungs, and around the heart where they pulsed like some sort of power taking possession.

Broadspeare listened with his whole body. So this is where my work had led. It is more beautiful, more wonderful than I ever imagined. His heart pounded in excitement until he realized something was wrong. The tone was off-key. The rhythms were off by a half-beat. The pattern was almost there, but not perfect. "It's wrong," he shouted. "It's wrong. The music of the ritual is off." He shook the guard free and rushed over to Dobrinski and tried to push him out of way. Blevins stepped in, grabbed Broadspeare and threw him across the cave back into the clutches of the guards.

"Dad! Dad!" shouted Welsey, "He's right. He knows what he's talking about. You've got to stop it now. Please!"

Blevins hurled an angry look at her. "Why should I listen to anything you have to say? You call me Dad now, but you tried to kill me a couple of days ago for his sake. Why should I trust you?"

"I think it's working," said Dobrinski in his cold, mechanical voice. "Look at the other seismograph readings." He pointed to a series of screens bearing labels for area towns. "Belleville's received a good shock. Granite City probably lost a few buildings."

"A natural form of urban renewal," said Blevins. "The insurance company will call it an act of God."

"The act of a mad man," said Felix. "You're nuts, Blevins. Maybe you got knocked in the head too many times playing football, I don't know. But you best let me and Welsey out of here before somebody gets hurt."

"Is that a threat, old man? Why should I care what happens to you? You stole my daughter's childhood. You stole my place."

"I didn't steal anything. You abandoned her."

"I should kill you for that. You want her so much, get over there with her."

The guards prodded Amsdorfer to his feet with the rifle muzzles. Skippy snarled and moved in to protect his master. Before he could attack, one of the guards shot him. Before the dog could collapse, the ground gave a tremendous shift, knocking Amsdorfer to his feet. "You shot my dog!"

"Shut up, old man, before you get it too. Dobrinski, what's going on?" demanded Blevins.

Dobrinski looked at Blevins, then at Broadspeare, and finally back to the screens. Frantically, he made adjustments as the sound from the loudspeakers turned from a growl to a howl. "I'm getting feedback, too much feedback. This isn't supposed to be happening."

Another shock rippled through the cave, careening from one fork to another like a blind bull trying to escape. The shock knocked everyone to their feet. They scrambled to their feet. The guards and workers nodded to each other and ran from the cave, dropping whatever was in their hands.

"Dimi," pleaded Tolkens, "we've got to get out of here." She tugged at his arm, pulling him over. He regained his balance and shook her off.

"Dobrinski, what the hell is going on here?"

"I don't know." He looked to Broadspeare and said, "You designed this thing. You said something isn't right. Tell me."

Before Broadspeare could move, Blevins snatched up one the rifles and pointed at him.

"Dimi, don't!" screamed Tolkens, grabbing his arm. "You've got to get me out of here."

Another shock wave, this one rattling up the cavern walls, knocking off stones and gashing a hole in the ceiling while chunks of rocks crushed down. Instinctively, everyone tried to cover their heads with their hands. When the rocks stopped falling, Dobrinski lay dead, his head crushed.

Tolkens screamed and Blevins slapped her. "Shut up! I'll get you out of here." He pulled her away from Dobrinski who she kept staring at, whimpering.

"Dad! What about us?"

"Don't worry, Daddy'll take care of his little girl when he comes back."

"Like hell you will. I'll take care of her like I always have," said Felix.

Blevins pointed the rifle at him and shot him. "Not this time. She's my daughter, not yours."

The next shock wave through the ceiling drove Blevins and Tolkens out of the cave. The lithographometer shrieked. The forks quivered in disharmony and the entrance collapsed into a pile of dust and rubble.

Troy stepped over Dobrinski's body and took over the lithographometer, swiping his hand over the screen. The shrieking stopped, but the tremors continued. The seismographs displaying rising Richter numbers spreading through the fault lines.

"We need to reset the forks. Welsey, I need your help."

What about Felix?" He lay with his head on her lap.

"Your father shot me up good. If I'm going to get out of here, it better be quick. Go help him."

Welsey left him and took her place at Troy's side.

"The ritual is wrong. We need what we heard in the churches—the deep, reverent tones." He took his hands off the screen and the screaming returned, setting off the forks and vibrations.

"Give me your hand. Place it here, right over this icon. Whatever happens, don't move," Troy said to her.

"What's going to happen?"

"I don't know. I only know what I would like to happen."

He followed the waves rippling through the floor like he was walking on water and took a stance in the middle of the forks, the only place of calm in the cave. He paused, closed his eyes and reached out with his mind for the vibrations running beneath his feet. Eyes still closed, he raised his arms and opened his mouth, letting the tones, letting the rhythm, letting the voice of the ancient priest-kings rise through his body and out. He cast himself into the ritual, opening and closing his mouth, moving his lips. Through his mind he saw the brilliance of the obsidian stone forks following his command, sending their waves deep into the ground. A change in tone and one set of shock waves retreated and another advanced. The rock became like clay in the hands of the potter. He turned his palms down, slowly lowering his arms and his voice.

The only sound in the cavern was the drops of water falling from the fingers of the fossilized hand into the pool at the bottom of the wall; the pool growing larger.

"You did it!" she cried. Her voice echoed through the cave like an announcement to the world.

"I wouldn't have believed it if I hadn't seen it with my own eyes," said Felix. "Maybe you're not such a bad feller after all, Troy."

"Coming from you, Felix, that means a great deal. Now we have figure out another way out of here, like the way we first came in."

Holding Felix between them, Troy and Welsey splashed through the rising water to the hole in the meadow. They could see the first light of dawn rising over Cahokia.

"This water wasn't here before, was it?" asked Troy.

"Maybe it's here because they cleared all the silt away."

The water dripping from the hand increased to steady flow.

"Shh. Do you hear that?" Felix asked. He pointed towards the opening. "It sounds like traffic on the highway." The low droning fell onto the ground and sent a wave across the pool of water that now lapped against the nearest fork. This set up a new vibration quickly followed by a second fork followed by a third responding in synchronous harmony.

"I thought you stopped it," said Welsey.

"So did I, but it looks like it's starting again. What did we do wrong?"

Felix groaned and sagged.

"Felix! Felix! Please tell me you're going to be all right. Please promise me," she said.

Felix put his arm around her and whispered through his groans, "Get me out of this water. I need to sit down." They pulled him back into the cave through the rising water to the highest spot. The light shining through the hole snapped and sparkled into the darkness.

"What did we do wrong? What was missing? The ritual was right, I know that. Welsey, what happened when we first come down here? What did we find?"

"The forks were all buried in the silt. That must have kept them from vibrating all these years.

"Yes, and you walked over here." He walked towards the largest fork.

"And I touched it and began to bleed."

"Then I saw the skulls and … oh, God, no." He looked at her and saw the tears in her eyes and he knew that she knew and neither wanted to say it. Behind their silence the water flow increased.

"You two don't want to say it, do you," said Felix. He took a shallow breath. He shifted over onto his hands and knees, and sagging and collapsing, drug himself the fork. "It needs blood."

"Felix, you can't. We need to get you out of here," she pleaded.

"Come here, girl. I'm all done in anyway. That shot tore up all my insides and I know it. There's only one thing, though. For all those years, I should have let you call me Popsie."

The vibrations shattered the rocks beneath them, sending shards popping off the floor. It went from one fork to another, setting them off in a cacophony of noise that turned into a lament that gathered strength.

"Popsie, tell me what to do."

"Lean me up against this fork. This thing wants blood and I've got a little left. Open my shirt."

She tore open his shirt and gasped at the size of the whole, blood flowing out of it. He opened his arms and embraced the obsidian pillar.

"I love you, Popsie."

"I love you, my own little girl. Now, let's get this over with." He raked his body up against the razor edges of the pillar, staining it red. Troy reached for Welsey and told her she had to join him.

Together they stood in the center of the forks, like the hub of a wheel. He clasped her hand, paused, and again felt the voice of the stones welling up through his feet. He guided it into her hand, her body, her feet until she, too, connected. Then they sang. They sang for Felix. They sang for each other. They sang for the world and as they sang, they felt the vibrations turn to the quiet of their song, their psalm. They turned the lament into a hymn of peace.

When they stopped the vibrations had all but stopped except for one spasm that shot out between their feet and headed for the wall, as if the fossilized hand was reaching for it, calling it home. When it hit the wall, the wall shattered and the torrent behind the wall broke free and the flood began.

"Can you swim?" he asked.

"Sort of. You?"

"About the same. Working together, we might make it."

They latched onto a large timber and tried to hang on but as the water rose, the timber sank. "Something's got to be holding it," said Welsey, struggling to keep one hand on the timber and her head above water. Troy dove and discovered the timber was anchored to the cave floor by a thick rope. When he came to the surface, he saw that the water was gaining on them. If they let loose of the timber, they'd be washed deeper into the cave. He remembered his pocket knife, pulled it out of his pocket, pulled the blade out with his teeth and dove again. The knife was duller than he had thought and he sawed against the rope. Finally, he cut the timber free. They clung to it and kicked against the current towards the light. By the time they reached it, the sun had risen well above the horizon and shone of the face of the stone with the glyphs sparkling in the sunlight.

"Climb up the rock," he said.

"I can't reach it."

"Let me try to push you up." He shoved her towards the stone and she grabbed on and clung to it.

"What about you?" she said as the waters swirled around him, the current pulling him back into the cave.

"I'll find a way," he yelled. The rising flood left only the tops of the forks above the water. An idea flashed through his mind, *it just might work*. He shifted to the end of the timber and using it like a kick board aimed for the first pair of fork tips. He kicked as hard as he could, aiming for them. He hit them and bounced off, quickly aiming for the second and struck them as hard as he could. Vibrations moved through his body when he aimed for the third and the fourth. Two more. Let me have strength. Barely able to kick his feet, he aimed for them, hit one and then nudged the other. It was enough.

The sonic harmony moved through the water and set the floor into a synchronic vibration, but lacking the full ritual, it ran chaotically. The weight of the water dampened it, but it was enough to send a fissure through the floor and the water poured through like a drain. He saw the forks rise through the water, casting their shadows on the water. Before long, his feet touch the muddy cavern floor. There was no sign of either Dobrinski or Felix.

He collapsed onto the floor into the damp ooze. At least he was on the ground. "Solid as a rock," he chuckled. A chill moved into his bones and he knew he had to get up, to move around. He rose and fell back down, flat on his back, then he saw a small circle of light moving across the cave wall, followed by his name being called.

"Dr. Broadspeare?"

He croaked a reply and feebly waved his hand. When the light shone in his eyes, the brightness forced him to shade his face with his hand.

Feet splashed through the standing pools, coming closer. "Dr. Broadspeare? I'm Agent Wagons with the Department of Homeland Security. We're here to get you out." Behind the agent stood a cadre of state troopers and a rescue team, flashing their lights all around the cave with the look of amazement.

"Wow. What is this place?"

"It's a place where the gods go to die."

As they were strapping him into a hoisting harness, the agent informed him that Welsey had called from Amsdorfer's house. "We could charge her with breaking and entering, But probably won't. We tried to take her to the hospital, but she refused to go until she knew you were safe and out of this place."

The harness hadn't been tied correctly and the straps chaffed under his armpits, but he was beyond caring. All he wanted was to be out of the pit. "Yes, the pit, that a good word for it, the pit," he muttered while they hoisted him up.

At the lip of the hole, he struggled to be free of the harness. In the bright light of day he saw her standing dressed in overalls and a flannel shirt she must have found in Felix' closet. He stumbled across the frost encrusted grass and into the blanket she held out in her open arms.

"What would Felix say about pulling me out of the drink again?"

"He would say you deserved to be saved." She began to sob and he held her until the February chill forced them off the meadow and into the house. By the time they reached the house, he had managed to soak her through and both shivered with teeth chattering. An EMT helped him into the bathroom and began pulling off his wet, muddy clothes. Feigning embarrassment, Troy hid the bullet wound from the EMT's sight.

Swathed in blankets, he went into the living room where the officers waited to take his statement. Welsey, also wrapped in blankets, sat alone on the couch. He sat down beside her and one of the officers handed him a cup. He tasted it—coffee laced with brandy.

"Dr. Broadspeare, do you feel strong enough to tell us your part of the story. Mrs. Yergens has already told us hers."

He glanced at her, wondering how complete she had been. Would they ever believe the real story about stopping the earthquake with song and a blood sacrifice? From the pleading of her soft, brown eyes, from the depth that shone forth from those eyes, from the wisdom that was beyond her years, he knew she hadn't. Instead of the truth, he told them a tale about an expedition gone wrong, about trying to save ancient Cahokia artifacts being stolen, about their attempts to protect an ancient site from ruin. He told them what was plausible, that Felix had been shot protecting the artifacts before the flood threw him against the obsidian pillars. As he told them his part of the story, he could feel the tension easing from Welsey's body.

They had told the same story and gave the same information. When he finished, one of the cave's rescue members entered carrying the mud encrusted lithographometer.

"We've pretty well examined the cavern. That flood cleaned it out. All we found were the busted-up Bobcat, the two bodies, and this." He held up the lithographometer. "Some kind of weird computer."

"It's mine," said Troy. "I used it for research. It was part of our testing equipment." He reached out to take it but was stopped by the officer in charge.

"We'll need it for the investigation." When he took it, water poured out from it. "If it's electronic, I doubt if it'll ever work again. Mark it as evidence."

The officer's phone rang. "They got them? All of them, the guards, too? Good." He put the phone away and looked at the pair on the couch. "If you'll excuse me, they need me back at the office. They caught the guards, Miss Tolkens, and your father, Mrs. Yergens." He sighed, "One hell of a day. Promise me you'll stick around in case I have any more questions. If not, I'll have to get an injunction." He nodded to the rest of the officers and they left. Before the last car could pull out of the driveway, exhaustion took over and Welsey and Troy fell asleep on the couch, wrapped in blankets and leaning against each other.

Troy cherished the honor of being one of the pall bearers at Felix's funeral, a funeral that packed the church. Former students from far and wide came to pay their respects to their old Latin teacher. When Welsey took the lectern and quoted, "*Non est ad astra mollis e terris via.*"* Troy watched the smiles of understanding that passed among so many of the mourners and realized the impact Felix had made on his students.

The trial for Blevins attracted even larger crowds, especially crews from the news media for never had a former Super Bowl star been indicted with such a long list of charges including accessory to murder, public endangerment, theft of archeological treasures, criminal trespass on state property, and so on. Both Troy and Welsey gave their testimony, and when she took the stand, her father refused to make eye contact, a detail picked up by the news. The trials for Tolkens and the guards attracted only a few of their family members. When the trials were over, Troy contacted Avon Greenefield and told her that he should be coming back to campus and that he was sure he could prove that his sabbatical was more than rewarding.

Felix, in his will, left the farm to the state of Illinois so Cahokia Mounds State Park could be expanded. On the night before Troy planned to leave, a fleet of trucks and crew of workers showed up on Felix's farm, drove across the meadow, and sealed up the hole with a concrete cover bearing a sign warning of criminal trespass, signed, "Department of Homeland Security."

"I don't know if I should be happy or sad about this," he said, pointing to the concrete cover.

"Why?"

"Whatever happened down there needs to be studied. It vindicates everything I've done, everything I've spent most of my life researching."

"But on the other hand."

"On the other hand, whatever happened down there should never happen again. It would best be completely forgotten about."

"That's not going to happen, will it?"

"No. Neither of us could ever let it rest. The full story needs to be written and published."

"In an authentic academic journal this time?" she asked with a slight raising of one eyebrow.

"Yes, an authentic journal. There might even be more, like a book, but not only for me, but for you as well." He slipped his hand into hers and pulled her closer.

"What are you driving at, Dr. Broadspeare?"

"I need your help, and not only for this project." He paused, looked off to Monk's Mound, and said, "But before I go on, I have to tell you that I can't stand calling you Mrs. Yergens."

"That's who I am."

"That's who you are now, but I would like to call you Mrs. Broadspeare. Come back with me. Work with me. Marry me. I love you, Welsey. I do. I realize I'm more than a bit older than you, and I don't have a lot to offer. I don't even have a place to live anymore. All I have is me."

"Mrs. Broadspeare, eh?"

"Yes, please."

"That would do for a while."

He pulled away from her. "What do you mean—a while?

"I think there should be room for more than one Dr. Broadspeare."

There is no easy way from the earth to the stars. (Seneca)

About the Author

Thomas Sabel was raised on a chicken farm near Grovertown, Indiana, served in the U.S. Army, has tended bar, performed Shakespeare, done carpentry, retired from the Lutheran ministry, and currently teaches college in Fort Wayne, Indiana where he lives with his wife of 30 years, Judith. His published works have appeared in *Hayday* Magazine, *Steam Ticket*, *Tipton Poetry Journal*, *riverrun Magazine*, and others. His novels include *Legends of Luternia: the Prince Decides* and *I is Dead*.

Acknowledgements

A special thanks to Liz Kramer who did a fantastic job of designing the cover.

Made in the USA
Columbia, SC
18 June 2023

17925652R00112